Praise for Janice Eidus'

Urban Bliss

"Brilliantly observant, relentlessly funny—smart, witty, vibrant—All can be said for the wonderful fiction of Janice Eidus and her charming character, Babette. I hated *Urban Bliss* to end and continue to wish that Babette lived next door. She's one in a million!"

—Jill McCorkle, author of *Carolina Moon*

"(A) whimsical, clean, and fast-paced read, both sexy and savvy, about punctured promises and deception . . . Eidus' seriously funny world (is) anything but safe."

—*The Review of Contemporary Fiction*

"Reading Urban Bliss is sheer pleasure—alive and cheeky and funny and smart (sweet too) without ever straining for any of its effects; plus its 90s Manhattanites are the best gang of eccentrics-with-an-edge this side of "Seinfeld." Ever since I discovered her fiction, I've been convinced that Janice Eidus is a bona-fide original and telling everyone to check out her work."

—Tom De Haven, author of *Derby Dugan's Depression Blues*

"We remember Eidus as the author of the striking short story collection *Vito Loves Geraldine* (1990); now we'll know her as a witty and satirical novelist. . . . Eidus has fashioned an amusingly jittery, arty, and madcap social scene, but behind this slick facade, she is actually examining the compromises intrinsic to marriage and exposing the turmoil generated by the confusion of fantasy with reality."

—Donna Seaman, *Booklist*

". . . a ruefully funny, observant tak~ ~~ ~~han ~n~~~."

y

Urban Bliss

Janice Eidus

CITY LIGHTS BOOKS
San Francisco

Originally published in hardcover by Fromm International Publishing
Corporation in 1994.

Cover Design by DiJiT

Library of Congress Cataloging-in-Publication Data

Eidus, Janice
    Urban Bliss   /   by Janice Eidus
  p.   cm.
    ISBN 0-87286-339-5
    1. City and town life —New York (State)—New York—
Fiction. 2. Marriage—New York—Fiction.   I. Title.
    (PS3555.I38U73   1998)
    813' .54—dc21   98-11041
                                                      CIP

City Lights Books are available to bookstores through our primary
distributor: Subterranean Company, P. O. Box 160, 265 S. 5th St.,
Monroe, OR 97456. Tel: (541)-847-5274. Toll-free orders
(800)-274-7826. Fax: (541)-847-6018. Our books are also available
through library jobbers and regional distributors. For personal orders
and catalogs, please write to City Lights Books, 261 Columbus Avenue,
San Francisco, CA 94133, or visit us on the World Wide Web at:
www.citylights.com.

CITY LIGHTS BOOKS are edited by Lawrence Ferlinghetti and
Nancy J. Peters and published at the City Lights Bookstore,
261 Columbus Avenue, San Francisco, CA 94133.

Once Again, for John

I would like to thank

my agent, Ellen Levine;
my editor, Thomas Thornton;
and Marnie Mueller,
    for their invaluable editorial suggestions;

Alice B. Acheson for her friendship and unflagging
    enthusiasm;

Bill Smart and the staff of The Virginia Center for the
    Creative Arts, for providing me a "home away from
    home" so many times;

Yaddo and Ragdale for my productive, stimulating
    residencies;

Audrey and Peter Kastan for The Atrium, which helps
    my creative juices to flow;

Joan Stein, for her support and wisdom;

and Jim Dixon and Mark Chambers, for twice helping
    me to create a "room of my own."

Urban (*adj*): characteristic of the city as distinguished from the country; citified.

Bliss (*noun*) **1**: great joy or happiness; **2**: spiritual joy; rapture; (*Slang*) to experience or produce ecstasy or intense pleasure or satisfaction from or as if from a hallucinogenic drug or a mystical experience: usually with*out*.

—*Webster's New World Dictionary*

"New York without the Arts Is Like a Picnic without the Ants."

Urban Bliss

1

"You've *got* to come back to work, Babette." Jay Adroit looks beseechingly at me. Jay is my boss. At this moment, he's sitting across from me in my sister's living room.

I shake my head. "No, Jay. You're the one who gave me the summer off. Don't forget, I have it in writing." I cross my legs, trying to get comfortable in my sister's oversize hot pink armchair, trying not to reveal the pangs of guilt that Jay's comment evokes in me.

"Babette, you're absolutely heartless." Jay looks mortally wounded.

His comment convinces me I've succeeded in not showing guilt. But I don't bother to reply, since it's not true. I've never been heartless: Even back when I was single, and I broke the heart of more than one man, I always felt guilty.

I do admit, however, that I can be flip at times. I can't help myself. My therapist says my flippancy is a defense and that I deal with my problems by acting like a stand-up comic.

My sister enters from the kitchen and sits next to Jay on the pink sofa. "That's not very nice, Babette," she admonishes in her older-sister tone, as she caresses the ruffle at the neck of her pink silk dress. Pink is her trademark. Everything that belongs to her is pink. She's an interior designer: The name of her firm is "Maya Bliss: Pretty in Pink."

Whenever I visit her, I avoid wearing that color. Today I'm in faded blue jeans and a pale blue sweater.

"TAG needs you," Jay says to me.

"What's TAG?" Maya's six-year-old daughter Alex tiptoes into the room, carrying a drawing pad and a box of crayons. Alex—who's wearing a pink sundress—plops herself down in the center of the rug.

Jay looks at Alex as though she's a philistine for not knowing that TAG, a.k.a. the Theater Art Gallery, is a theater for performance artists, playwrights, musicians, and dancers whose work is much too "cutting edge" for Broadway, off Broadway, and, in most cases, even off-off-Broadway. Together, without any other staff, Jay and I run TAG. I'm the associate director, and Jay is both director and founder.

"TAG is a theater," I tell Alex. "People perform there." "That's true, Alex," Jay says, "but what your heartless Aunt Babette is neglecting to tell you, because she just doesn't care enough, is that a bunch of mean, nasty, terrible men want to destroy TAG."

Wide-eyed, Alex looks up at Jay.

"These nasty men hate old buildings," Jay continues, ignoring the irritated look I'm giving him, "and they want to murder TAG just because it's located in an old building. They want to tear the building down and replace it with a brand-new condominium monster, which, depending on the economy, they may not even be able to fill!"

"A condominium, sweetie," I explain to Alex, in my most reassuring tone, hoping that Jay hasn't frightened her with his wild talk about murder and monsters, "just means an apartment that someone owns, that's all, except it's different from a co-op, which is what you and your mommy live in, like lots of people on the Upper East Side these days…"

"I'm going to draw you, Aunt Babette," Alex cuts me off, losing interest in the conversation. She doesn't appear frightened.

"Your Aunt Babette and I will both lose our jobs if TAG is torn down," Jay mutters, "and if it weren't for the fact that her husband is a successful corporate lawyer, she'd be as worried as I am, and she'd cut short her absurdly long vacation—which I was much too kind to allow her to take!—in order to help me fight Acme Developers."

Again, I rearrange my position in the uncomfortable armchair and try not to evince any emotion at Jay's words, even though I *am* very, very worried about being permanently unemployed if TAG is torn down. And I'm feeling guiltier than ever.

Alex nods, as though Jay's babble has made perfect sense to her. She looks down, chooses a crayon from the box, and begins to draw.

2

Despite my guilt, I refuse to work at TAG this summer for the following reason: I'm having a crisis. Or, more accurately, I'm having three crises. So, before I knew about Acme Developers' plans to tear down TAG's funky old tenement home on Tenth Avenue and 57th Street—which is one block from where I live—I'd arranged to take the entire summer off to deal with my own crises.

Crisis Number One concerns adultery, and my very painful suspicions about George, my husband.

Crisis Number Two concerns the confusing subject of motherhood, and whether or not it's for me.

And Crisis Number Three concerns TAG itself, and the fact that my work there no longer satisfies me.

Maya, who's unaware of any of my three crises, straightens the paisley scarf around her neck. She takes out a compact and reapplies her rosy pink lipstick, until she just about blends into the sofa.

Alex looks up from her drawing. "Mommy," she announces, "you and Jay don't match. You're like plaid and polka dots."

Maya's embarrassed. Jay's annoyed. And I silently marvel at how insightful Alex is in spotting how ill-matched they are as a couple. I still can't believe Jay called Maya up one night six weeks ago and asked her to have dinner with him, and that ever since then they've been an "item." Pinky pink Maya, with her sprayed blond hair, looks as though she's bound to have a couple of rich old sugar daddies always hanging around catering to her every whim. And Jay, short, skinny, and balding, with wire-rimmed glasses that constantly slide down his nose, and baggy suit jackets and flowered bow ties, is the furthest thing in the world from a doting old sugar daddy. Besides, I also know for a fact that Maya's no fan of TAG's. "Babette," she's said to me, on more than one occasion, "why do you waste your time with all that weird theater? You should work for a theater that puts on shows that _real_ people like."

"Alex," Maya says, interrupting my thoughts about her taste— or lack of it—in theater, "why don't you go to your room and work on your act?"

"That's a good idea," Jay agrees. "What act?"

Maya rolls her eyes. "Alex told me earlier that she's been working up some sort of act that she wants to perform for all of us later. So really, Alex, go off and...create."

Alex meets her mother's ferocious gaze.

"Alex is creating right now," I admonish Maya and Jay. "She's drawing my portrait."

"Yes, that's wonderful," Maya says, annoyed with me, "but Alex honey, as soon as you're done drawing Aunt Babette, you'll go to your room, won't you?" She turns to me. "And by the way, Aunt Babette, just how late is your husband planning to be tonight?" She looks at her watch to make her point.

I cringe, despite my resolve not to show vulnerability in front of Jay and Maya. I'm certain that Maya has already figured out that George isn't joining me here tonight, which means she's asking just to get back at me for interfering on Alex's behalf.

"Yeah, we could use George's keen legal mind to help us figure out how to save TAG," Jay says.

"Look," I point at the pile of crayons Alex has assembled next to her on the rug, "don't you think Alex has an excellent eye for color?"

"Babette, where's George?" Maya persists.

"At the office." I'm unable to keep the tension out of my voice. "Working late." I can't be flip, much as I'd like to be, about George's absence. Not in the midst of the Adultery Crisis.

Jay is staring at me, and I can just about see the light bulb go off over his head as he puts it all together: George is absent; Babette is alone; Babette is tense. He practically snaps his fingers. I'm sure he's remembering that the reason I asked him for the summer off from TAG in the first place was because of my suspicion that George is having an affair.

The only reason I'd ever confided in Jay was because I figured that somewhere, deep inside of him, an iota of empathy must exist. He hadn't been so thrilled when his own wife, who'd been having an affair, ended up leaving him a few years ago. I must have figured right, because he did give me the summer off. He agreed not to tell Maya about my suspicions, and I was sure I could trust him on *that* score, not because of his loyalty to me but because he's too self-centered to remember anyone else's problems for very long.

Alex rises from the rug and climbs gracefully onto my lap. "Look, Aunt Babette," she says, holding out her drawing, "you!"

Although she has colored my face an unnaturally bright orange, like a Halloween pumpkin, she's managed to color my hair and eyes a realistic, true-to-life chocolate brown. And she's also rendered very well the shape of the Veronica Lake bodywave my hairdresser gave me last week, complete with the hair-falling-over-one-eye vamp routine.

Alex points to a much smaller head in the bottom left corner of the page. "That's Mommy." She's drawn Maya entirely in yellow: yellow hair, yellow lips, yellow eyes. I smile, seeing this as a healthy sign of rebellion.

"Let me see, honey," Maya says.

Alex climbs down from my lap and trots across the rug to Maya.

"Very creative." Maya looks at the drawing with a pained expression. "But we're going to have to take you to an ophthalmologist to check for color blindness."

"I'm not color-blind," Alex says. "I know that red means stop, green means go, pink means Mommy, and blue means Aunt Babette."

3

Alex climbs back onto my lap. I stroke her shiny blond hair and marvel again at how insightful and talented she is, and how she'll be able to be anything she wants to be when she grows up—a great actress, a great artist, or, judging by her yellow drawing of Maya, a great leader of social rebellions.

I continue to stroke Alex's hair, and I find myself thinking about my motherhood crisis. I feel teary-eyed, which is the last thing I want to feel around Jay and Maya. When we were kids, Maya made fun of me for being a crybaby. "For such a snotty wiseass, Babette," she would say, "you're really just a little crybaby."

Nowadays, my therapist tells me that I easily go back and forth between being insouciant and weepy because I'm the "volatile type." So, volatile type that I am, I sit here stroking Alex's hair, holding back my tears, and I can't help wondering whether I want a child of my own. Maybe. I'm not sure. But I'm thirty-five years old, a year younger than Maya, and my biological clock *is* ticking away. I don't have a huge amount of time left to decide. But how can I consider having George's child if he's having an affair, and if I don't even know what I want to do with the rest of my life?

"Aunt Babette," Alex announces, "now I'll draw you in blue." She climbs down from my lap and seats herself comfortably once again on the rug.

"You know, darling, you might try drawing your Aunt Babette in her real-life skin color this time," Maya says.

"TAG is in crisis," Jay announces, trying to bring us back to the only subject on his mind.

The phone rings in the bedroom.

"Probably a client." Maya sounds eager. Her silk dress rustles as she rises and steps lightly across the furry rug, heading toward her bedroom.

"Babette," Jay turns to me, "how can you just abandon me?" I shrug, wishing I could come up with an appropriately witty, wiseass retort.

Maya returns, clearly disappointed. "It's for you," she says to me. "It's George."

I walk slowly into Maya's bedroom. I sit on the satin bedspread and pick up the trim cordless telephone.

"Hi," George says, sounding insincerely cheerful, just like Maya's all-pink bedroom. "I want to apologize again for not being able to meet you tonight."

"Working away on an urgent case, I presume?" Once again, I try to sound unconcerned. It's becoming a habit, not revealing my true feelings to anyone.

"Right." He sounds uncomfortable.

George has been working late at the office nearly every night for months. And for some reason, there's always just one other lawyer working late with him—Nicole Burden, the tall, blond granddaughter of one of the firm's founders.

"Fine, George. I'll give everyone your best." I have no energy to confront him and, even if I did, I could never do it in a pink room.

I hang up before he can say anything else, if in fact he was going to bother to say anything else. George has always been the thoughtful silent type, as opposed to the macho silent type. When I first met him, his silences seemed seductive to me, like unfathomable mysteries. But lately they're just painful, filled with unspoken lies.

Not ready to return to Jay's hysterics about TAG, I stare at a framed photo on the bureau next to the bed. It's of Maya, myself, and my parents. Maya and I are about Alex's age. We're in a playground in the Bronx, standing in front of the swings. My mother is holding Maya's hand; my father is holding mine. Maya and I look too sweet and innocent for words, and I know that Maya was never really that sweet and innocent. I probably wasn't either. My mother's hair is pinned on top of her head in a curly bun, and she looks like Lucy Ricardo, wide-eyed and wacky, while my father, balding even then, looks like a trimmer Fred Mertz. These days, they're enjoying their golden years in Woodstock, organizing letter-writing campaigns for Amnesty International and taking pottery classes. I wonder, not for the first time, how Maya and I, from the same Jewish liberal middle-class Bronx roots, have turned out so different. Maya sees the world through a pair of rosy pink glasses she refuses to remove, while I refuse to put those glasses on, even for a second.

"I want to do my act in here, right now!" Alex is insisting, when I return to the living room. She's abandoned her blue portrait of me.

"Later," Maya tells her, in a firm tone. "First, we're going to have a long talk with Uncle Jay."

"He's *not* my uncle," Alex mutters.

"Oh, Maya, come on, let her do her act," I interrupt, even though I know that being an aunt doesn't really allow me to keep contradicting Maya.

"TAG," Jay leaps to his feet, "is in hot water! Soon TAG shall be homeless, and its visionary theater artists shall be stranded and alone unless *you*," he looks at me, and then Maya, "help me to do something now!" Quickly, while he has our attention, he rises from the sofa and walks to the center of the room. He spreads his arms wide, and intones, in the manner of a southern TV evangelist, "I have a responsibility. And you do, as well. Acme Developers has us by the b—" He remembers Alex. "By the behind," he says, like an embarrassed, censored TV evangelist.

I laugh, charmed by Jay's theatrics, in spite of myself.

"Behind," Alex repeats, giggling and looking at Maya, whose surprised expression tells me that she's seeing a side of Jay she hasn't seen before, a side she may need time to get used to.

"Help! The evil condominium monster is going to eat up all the theater artists of New York City!" Jay shouts, abandoning the evangelist act and playing directly to Alex.

"What does the condominium monster look like?" Alex asks. Jay begins to do an imitation of the mummy, from the old movie of the same name. He walks around Maya's pink living room with an exaggerated limp, one arm outstretched, and a demented expression on his face.

Alex giggles, but Maya, fingering her scarf, looks appalled.

Abruptly, Jay stops the mummy act. He sits back down on the sofa. "Seriously, Babette, if you don't help, you'll have on your conscience for the rest of your life the misery and destitution of all these artists who are so ahead of their time they'll have nowhere to perform once TAG is gone!"

"Oh, come on, Jay, it's not as bad as that. We'll find another home for TAG." But even as I say it, my voice shakes, because homelessness—like my suspicions about George's adultery—is another subject I can't be flip about. It doesn't seem to matter whether the real-estate market is hard or soft or whether the economy is up or down, homelessness in this city appears to be here to stay. Dishwashers and college professors alike can't pay their rent. And plenty of arts organizations—and artists—are already homeless. Jay isn't lying. He knows what he's talking about. Still, I feel determined not to set foot at TAG this summer. If I allow myself to get too involved in TAG's crisis, I'll never deal with my own. And if I don't "confront things right now," as my therapist says, before I know it, Nicole Burden and George will have run off together and I'll be sixty years old, alone, too old even to adopt a child should I decide I really want one, and as confused as ever about what to do with the rest of my life.

From the pocket of his baggy jacket, Jay pulls out a videotape. "May I?" he asks Maya.

"Of course," Maya smiles. I'm sure she's relieved that Jay's mummy routine is finished. To Alex she says, "Uncle Jay is going to show us a movie. Isn't that fun?"

This inspires Alex to giggle even more. She's probably realizing that Jay is somewhat mad, something I figured out the first day I began working at TAG.

Jay walks across the room to where Maya's television sits on a pink table. With a grand flourish, he sticks the tape into the VCR. Before he switches the machine on, he turns to us. "This tape is Exhibit A. After viewing this tape, ladies and gentlemen of the jury, you will understand more fully why you must devote yourself to helping my client." Now he's playing an earnest lawyer in the courtroom.

Maya's still smiling. She's not as appalled by Jay's lawyer routine as by his mummy routine. It isn't too difficult to figure out why—lawyers earn more money than mummies.

Jay turns the machine on, and the tape begins. Exhibit A turns out to be an early tape of Lydia Smart, TAG's most successful performer. Lydia is onstage doing an extremely accurate Elvis Presley imitation, wearing a skin-tight gold lamé suit, strumming a flashy guitar, and swiveling her pelvis. Behind her, on a screen, flash images of starving third-world children.

"This piece is called *Nero Fiddles While Rome Burns*," Jay informs Alex, "and it's about how too many people are indifferent to the plight of the world's poor."

Wide-eyed, Alex stares at the screen.

Maya, however, is busy inspecting her high-heeled shoes. Maya's not a fan of Lydia Smart's. "She's just too confrontational," she explained to me once, turning down my offer of free tickets to a performance by Lydia. "Art should be…pleasant, palatable, you know, Babette, easy to take."

Lydia Smart—who definitely isn't "easy to take"—stops singing and gyrating. She grins savagely into the camera, and the tape ends.

"Remember, Babette," Jay says, oblivious to Maya's lack of interest in Lydia, "TAG was the only theater that let Lydia perform that piece. We can't go under!" Now he doesn't sound like anyone other than a highly agitated arts administrator named Jay Adroit.

"I've got an idea," Maya bursts out, looking up from her shoes. "You can write a letter to the Mayor, telling him he simply can't abandon the true artists of the city!"

I'm shocked. Maya must care about Jay a lot more than I imagined, for her even to try to come up with anything that might help TAG.

"Maya, that's a great idea," Jay says. "Babette, you'll draft the letter to the Mayor tomorrow morning, first thing."

"I will not! I don't know how many times I have to remind you that I'm on my summer vacation."

Jay sneers. "Summer vacation, *schmummer* vacation."

"Besides," I continue, "as you must both recall, Babette is the one who absolutely hates to write. Anything. Even letters. Especially letters to the Mayor." It's true. I have what my therapist calls "acute writing anxiety," which she says is also related to Crisis Number Three—my lack of fulfillment at TAG—although I'm not convinced about that part. But whatever it's related to, I *hate* writing. I'll make a thousand phone calls in one morning, rather than write one memo. There's something about seeing my words committed to paper that scares me, as though once something is written down, it's no longer mine. I'm like the members of those tribes who believe their souls are stolen from them when someone snaps their photograph.

"Babette," Maya goes on, inspired, "you should also organize a big demonstration for TAG!"

Jay continues to look at her adoringly. I see an image of Maya in a pink floor-length gown and Jay in a baggy tuxedo marching side by side down the aisle.

"You two go right ahead and organize a demonstration," I tell them. "I promise to come and carry a sign."

Alex stands up. "Okay, you all talked and talked and *talked.* Now it's my turn to do my act!" Without giving Maya a second to protest, she begins to dance in the middle of the room, a cross between a graceful ballet and down-home clogging. Her blond hair flies up and down. "My act," she huffs, completing a bouncy pirouette, "is called *Alex Does It.*"

Whirling to a stop in front of Jay, she pleads, "Oh, Uncle Jay, please let me perform *Alex Does It* at TAG!"

Jay smiles. Finally, he's being called *Uncle* Jay. "Alex, *if* your Aunt Babette Bliss can help me save TAG—then you've got yourself a gig."

Now Jay has one more reason to make me feel guilty if I don't go back to work at TAG this summer.

I stand up. I've had it. Too much guilt and angst for one night. "I've got to go. I've got an appointment with Shara-Rose early tomorrow morning."

"Who's Shara-Rose?" Alex asks.

"Why, darling, she's Aunt Babette's therapist," Maya tells her. Although Maya disapproves of Shara-Rose, she doesn't say another word about her as she sees me to the door. I'm certain that this is because "Uncle Jay" also just happens to be a patient of Shara-Rose's.

4

I first met Shara-Rose at TAG, shortly after I'd been hired by Jay to work there. She was in the audience watching Lydia Smart, who was doing a performance piece about the horrors of being a fat teenage girl, which she swears she was. Lydia was onstage miming a binging episode and singing an original song called "Fat Girls Eat It in America Today."

Shara-Rose was sitting by herself in the back row, and I noticed her right away. For one thing, she has bright red curly hair, and for another, she was wearing lime green leather pants. She was also smoking, even though there were about five "No Smoking" signs up. And she was speaking very intensely into a tape recorder. I tiptoed up behind her to hear what she was saying. "Fat girls eat it up," she said in a raspy chainsmoker's voice.

"Excuse me," I said, "what are you doing?"

She turned around. "Thanks for interrupting me," she said loudly and sarcastically, in a thick Queens accent, blowing smoke in my direction. "What I'm doing, obviously, is repeating what Lydia Smart is saying into my tape recorder."

"Yes, I can see that," I answered coolly, refusing to allow myself to be intimidated. I already admired her for the lime green leather pants, and—as a former wild kid from one of "the boroughs," myself—I felt simpatico with her accent. "What I meant is, what in the world for? Since obviously Lydia thought of it first."

She smiled, suddenly and warmly. I had the feeling that she was admiring me, too, for standing up to her.

"Yeah, well," she said, "I'm a psychotherapist and I'm also the lead singer in a rock band called Mild Neurosis, and I'm gathering material about unhappy teenagers for both careers. Lydia Smart is material." She handed me her card. "Shara-Rose," it read, "Psychotherapist/Singer."

"I'm Babette Bliss," I offered, pocketing her card and looking at my watch at the same time. The performance was almost over, which meant I had to go backstage. "Nice meeting you."

I didn't think about her again until the following week, when Maya and I were having dinner together at Armstrong's, on Tenth Avenue. I'd suggested Armstrong's because it was cheap, and during my single days, I was always broke. I looked across the restaurant and saw Shara-Rose sitting at a table in the No Smoking section and lighting a cigarette. She wasn't alone.

The man with Shara-Rose immediately reminded me of George Harrison of the Beatles, heartthrob of my innocent, virginal, prepubescent years. Like Beatle George, this man was thin and wiry, with dark hair, slightly crooked teeth, thick eyebrows, and dark, intense eyes. One of my recurrent girlhood fantasies came back to me: I'm sitting by myself, lost in a sea of screaming girls, watching the Beatles perform onstage. Most of the other girls in the audience are either in love with Paul, the pretty one, or John, the witty one, or Ringo, the homely, vulnerable one. George, less pretty, less witty, less homely and vulnerable—mostly just quiet and distracted-looking—strums his guitar. His eyes roam idly through the large theater until they meet mine, and—whammo!—we fall in love at first sight.

Shara-Rose seemed to spot me at exactly the same moment I

spotted her. She grinned and waved wildly at me as if we'd been best friends since childhood. She said something to the George Harrison look-alike. He nodded, and she rose from her seat and strode over to my table. Conversation at other tables stopped; everyone in the restaurant was staring at Shara-Rose, who was wearing the lime green leather pants again, this time tucked into matching lime green cowboy boots.

Maya, too, was staring at Shara-Rose, as though she couldn't quite believe that this creature was coming over to us.

"Babette Bliss, the TAG lady," Shara-Rose greeted me. "Shara-Rose, this is my sister Maya," I said politely, "and Maya, this is Shara-Rose."

"Come have a drink with us." Shara-Rose sounded insistent.

Maya gave me a dirty look, which I knew was to remind me that she'd been in the midst of pouring her heart out to me, for the ten millionth time, about her unhappy marriage to Merv, whom I couldn't stand. Luckily for everyone, Merv ended up leaving Maya three years later for a nineteen-year-old showroom model.

"Shara-Rose, we'd love to join you," I declared, already determined to meet the George Harrison look-alike at Shara-Rose's table, despite Maya.

Maya gave me an even dirtier look, but she stood up with me and followed Shara-Rose back to her table. A number of the men at the bar who'd been watching Shara-Rose now turned their attention to Maya, who was flouncing petulantly along in her pink silk pants suit. I followed, and even though compared to both Shara-Rose and Maya I cut a subtle figure in my blue jeans and black turtleneck, I noticed that a number of the men were now staring at me. But I didn't care about any of those men: I only wanted to be sure that the man at Shara-Rose's table was looking at me, and he was.

Shara-Rose pushed two tables together. I deliberately chose the seat across from the George Harrison look-alike, so that I could stare directly into those dark brown eyes.

"Babette and Maya Bliss, I'd like you to meet George Harrison," Shara-Rose announced.

I felt mortified. Somehow, Shara-Rose had read my mind about my girlhood crush on Beatle George and was making fun of me.

But the man looked into my eyes with exactly the same brooding intensity with which Beatle George had looked into my eyes in my girlhood fantasy. "It's true," he said. He spoke carefully and softly. "Not only do I look like the Beatle, that really is my name."

Before I'd even had a second to digest all this, Shara-Rose looked at me and said, "George and I are pals, not lovers," as though I'd come right out and asked.

Although I felt even more mortified, I also felt relieved that she and the non-Beatle George Harrison were just friends.

Maya was looking increasingly annoyed, and I suspected that she too had begun to discern my interest in George Harrison.

The waitress, a bouncy, pigtailed type, came over. "So, what'll it be?" she asked.

I agreed to share a pitcher of beer with Shara-Rose and George. Maya ordered a Pink Lady.

"I never liked the Beatles," Maya offered sullenly.

This wasn't news to me, of course. As a kid, I used to peek at Maya's diary when she was out, and I was always coming upon entries like "My Dearest Diary, my little sister Babette is so silly, liking those dumb Beatles, especially that twirpy George Harrison!!!"

"Who was your favorite Beatle, Babette?" Shara-Rose asked. She lit a cigarette, took a puff, and obliviously blew smoke right at Maya, who was sitting across from her.

I hesitated. "My favorite Beatle was..." I hesitated again, "...George." Suddenly reckless, I added, "I absolutely adored him." I felt too shy to meet the non-Beatle George's eyes. Just being around this George Harrison look-alike had reduced me to the shy, blushing innocence of my prepubescence. Again, I didn't mind, particularly since I hadn't felt all that innocent for quite a while, being involved with two men at the time—one a wealthy, arrogant sculptor who I suspected had a drinking problem, and the other a sweet-but-chronically-depressed ad writer. The sculptor had a cynical, jaded charm, and the ad writer had a boyish, vulnerable charm, but neither seemed to me as charming as George Harrison, even though I'd just met him. It was exciting to feel like a blushing schoolgirl again.

"Well, in my case," Shara-Rose went on, "Ringo was my heart's desire, which makes it very easy for me and George here to remain such good platonic friends. Right, George?"

I was starting to have the distinct impression that Shara- Rose, for some reason known only to her, was doing a little matchmaking. But again, I didn't mind, whatever her reasons.

George smiled affectionately at her. "Right." Then he smiled at me.

I loved his smile, the way one tooth in front was slightly chipped, and the way his dark eyes seemed to gleam when he smiled. I knew I was far gone already.

The waitress brought our drinks. George poured the beer, and it took all my willpower not to reach over and rest my hand on his and ask him to tell me the entire story of his life, and not to leave out a single detail. I was already more interested in him than in the sculptor and the ad writer combined. Instead, I watched him take a sip of his beer. Trying to be witty, I asked, "So, were you born in Liverpool?"

George smiled, looked into the distance for a moment, and then spoke. I found the softness of his voice both seductive and compelling, and I leaned forward to hear. "I was born and raised on a farm in Sioux City, Iowa," he said. "And after I graduated from law school," he took another sip of his beer and stared at me, "I was struck with New York fever. To this day, I'm not sure why. Something about destiny. I felt that if I didn't move to New York, I'd never forgive myself. It was an obsession. I got the first job I applied for, at Burden, Lawrence, Shapiro, and O'Reilly, and I arrived, a shy farm boy, in a city filled with bigmouthed nonstop talkers."

Shara-Rose nodded, and leaned toward me, tapping her cigarette ash into her empty beer glass. "Really," she laughed, "the first day he came to group, he didn't say a word."

"Group?" I asked.

"That's how we met," Shara-Rose explained. "George and I were in a therapy group together. I was working on building up the courage to become a shrink myself, and George wanted to learn to talk loud and fast, to be tough and arrogant, the way he perceived New Yorkers to be."

"Because," George added, "back then, I equated loudness, toughness, and arrogance with success. And I very much wanted to be a successful lawyer."

"He walked into group the first day," Shara-Rose continued, "nodded at everyone with this faraway look in his eyes, sat in a corner, and just listened to the rest of us blah-blahing, and he didn't say a word. I figured he was mute."

"And," George said, "thanks to the loudmouths like Shara-Rose in the group, I learned that I can never be that way. I still count to ten before I allow myself to get angry. I still think that if you can't say something nice about somebody, you shouldn't say anything at all." He looked slightly sheepish. "And when push comes to shove, I still prefer peace and quiet. Silence still comforts me."

"Yeah," Shara-Rose said, again obliviously blowing smoke right at Maya and ignoring Maya's furious expression, "we all find certain things from our childhoods comforting. I like to wear pink nail polish because my mother used to reward me for being a good girl by letting me wear her Perfect Pink polish." She held out her hands. The fingernails on her left hand were painted bright pink. The fingernails on her right hand were painted black.

"Maya, look, Shara-Rose is also an aficionado of pink," I said, tearing my eyes away from George, hoping that this bond might ease relations between them.

"Except for pink furniture," Shara-Rose added happily. "The sight of it makes me nauseous."

Maya turned white. The time had definitely come for us to go. Maya was liable to do anything: toss her drink into Shara-Rose's face, bawl me out at the table, or most likely, sit there so sullenly that the rest of the evening would be ruined for everyone anyway. Besides, she _was_ my older sister, her marriage was in trouble, and she did need me, even if it was just as a sounding board. "Listen," I said apologetically to Shara-Rose and George, "Maya and I have to go."

Before the words were out of my mouth, Maya had paid her share of the check and was buttoning her coat.

Reluctantly, I also stood, put some money on the table, and slipped on the pale pink jacket Maya had given me as a birthday gift two years before, and which I'd never worn until that evening. I'd finally worn it out of guilt, since I was feeling so sorry for her about Merv.

Shara-Rose gave us both a hearty good-bye. George rose and shook my hand. The touch of his fingers made me giddy and weak.

Even more reluctantly, I followed Maya out the door of Armstrong's and down the block into a Greek coffee shop, where she proceeded to tell me two hours' worth of horror stories about Merv: He splattered toothpaste on the bathroom mirror; he never listened to a word Maya said; he refused to diaper his own daughter; he sometimes didn't come home until five in the morning, with no explanation. But all I could think about was George Harrison.

I was relieved when, after four cups of coffee, Maya called the Greek waiter over and asked for the check.

I saw her into a taxi, kissed her cheek, and said in what I hoped was a comforting tone, "Whatever happens between you and Merv, and I mean _whatever_, it'll probably be for the best."

Slowly I walked home along Broadway, trying to imagine what it would feel like to be held in George Harrison's arms.

When I arrived home, I was greeted at the door of my apartment by Flaca, my cat, whom I'd found on the street when she was a starving little kitten. My father, who was learning to speak Spanish by record at the time, took one look at her and said, "*Pobre Flaca*," and the name took. Flaca, who's no longer even slightly skinny, followed me into my bedroom. I slipped out of the pink jacket, and tossed it to the floor; now that I'd worn it once, maybe I could give it to the Salvation Army without feeling guilty.

I got into my nightgown, fed Flaca, snuggled beneath my covers, and dreamt all night long about both George Harrisons: the Beatle, and the one I'd just met across the table at Armstrong's. And in my dreams, I kept making wild love, back and forth, with both of them, twisting out of the arms of one, into the arms of the other, and then back into the arms of the first, madly happy in whichever set of arms I happened to land.

And when I awoke, what I decided to do was this: call Shara-Rose the very next morning, get the non-Beatle George's phone number, and then invite him to the next performance of *Fat Girls Eat It in America Today*, which was only two nights away. Then, after Lydia had taken her last bow to what in those days was always a nearly empty auditorium, I would entice him back to my apartment and seduce him. I had no time to waste: Any single man in New York City who looked that good—as handsome and moody as the spiritual Beatle, and bestowed by the hand of Fate with the exact same name, no less—had to be moved upon quickly. And I was determined that, once he set foot into my apartment, my seduction of him would be no ordinary seduction. It would be so romantic, so intense, that it would lead to true love for both of us. I would be so wild, uninhibited, and imaginative in bed with him that I would lead him to places that the girls back home in Sioux City hadn't even known existed. And yet I also would be the most sublimely receptive female he had ever encountered. Whatever he wanted done for him, I would do; and whatever he wanted to do for me, I would receive with both passion and grace, simultaneously. I could hardly wait: My prepubescent fantasy about Beatle George was destined to come true, at last!

5

"I'm not kidding, I want you to keep a journal this summer," Shara-Rose insists. She's wearing a black leather miniskirt and black tights, and she's sitting across from me in her office in one of those sleek Danish backless chairs.

I'm wearing the same old blue jeans and sweatshirt I wore to Maya's apartment last night. Shara-Rose's office is decorated, naturally, in leather, and I'm sitting in her big black leather armchair. "Shara-Rose, come off this journal kick." My tone is surly. "You know how much I hate to write. I took off from TAG this summer in order to figure out a practical strategy for dealing with my crises, not to keep a sentimental, girlish little diary." Despite my surly tone, it's really a relief to be someplace where I can let my true feelings show, even if they're not the most pleasant feelings in the world.

"Journal-keeping *is* therapeutic," Shara-Rose insists again, lighting a cigarette, the fourth she's smoked since my session began twenty-five minutes ago. "Writing your thoughts down can help you to gain insight about your feelings toward George and the possibility

that he's having—or not having—an affair with Nicole Burden.
And your feelings about motherhood. And about TAG and your
career and that unfocused yearning you claim to feel, and yet which
you're not willing to confront."

Shara-Rose says that she's used journal therapy with lots of her
patients, ranging from kleptomaniacs to emotionally unavailable
men, and it never fails. "Listen," she continues, "don't think of
what you write as journal entries. Imagine that you're just tossing
off friendly little letters to me, filled with your most intimate
details." Her eyes are glinting, which means she's having a good
time. "You can address them to 'Dear Shrink...'"

"I see you twice a week and I tell you all my deepest secrets.
Why would I need to 'toss off' friendly little letters to you?"

She stubs out her half-finished cigarette in an ashtray that's so
full it looks as though it hasn't been cleaned in days, although my
guess is that she's already emptied it at least once this morning.
She taps her nose, which usually means she's just had an inspira-
tion. "Look, if you think that keeping a journal is such a girlish
thing to do, why don't you get into the spirit entirely and address
the entries to your old heartthrob, Beatle George Harrison? I
mean, after all this time, you still sort of half-believe you're _really_
married to him, anyway, don't you?" She grins mischievously.

I know what she's getting at. She's always riding me that I "idealize" George too much, and that I still, after all this time, frequently expect him to be as perfect as my girlhood fantasy version
of Beatle George.

"Shara-Rose," I always answer, whenever she starts up with this
"idealization" stuff, "I wish you would get it through your head
once and for all, that I'm no longer a giggling little girl with a
crush on a rock star! I've been around the block more than a couple of times since then, and I know exactly who my husband is.
He's a lawyer. It's true, in the very beginning, when I first met him,
I had some erotic dreams starring both of them together. But I'm

very, very clear on who he is by now, don't worry. My George can't even play the guitar!"

This time, I don't even bother answering. She and I sit in silence for a while. She smokes, I bite my fingernails.

Finally she says, "Okay, that's it."

Usually I'm sorry when our sessions are over, but today I'm grateful. I'm so irritated by her stupid journal-therapy kick, her insistence that I break through my writing anxiety, and also the fact that she keeps bringing up this business about my still being a "groupie" who's unable to distinguish between her own adulterous husband and a Beatle. I begin to question my decision—made shortly after I first moved into George's midtown apartment and we decided to get married—to begin therapy with her. It had something to do with my wanting to lead "the examined life." I must have been as crazy as she is. She sees me to her door. "Write well," she says, blowing smoke in my direction. In the hall, I ring for the elevator. Shara-Rose's office is in a musty old apartment building that used to be a hotel. Now it's filled with elderly women on fixed incomes and raucous college students whose schools rent whole floors as dorm space. I wonder if there's any available space in the building large enough to house TAG.

The elevator arrives. Jay steps out.

"I deliberately asked her," he points at Shara-Rose's door, "for the session after yours, Babette." He's breathing fast, and his voice is tight and high-pitched. "You ran out on me last night."

He's standing in the elevator doorway, blocking it so I can't get in.

"Jay," I try to stay calm, but my voice is rising, "you've got all the other tenants in the building helping you to fight Acme Developers. You know that. You're hardly alone in this."

"I want *you* to help," he says, pushing his glasses up, and giving me what I suspect he thinks is a winning, boyish look.

"Sorry. I really am. But I can't do it. You know how upset I am about George." I wait to see if he responds to my reminding him that I, too, am having a crisis. He doesn't, so I go on. "Besides, Shara-Rose wants me to keep a journal this summer, and that's more than enough work for me."

"Well, it just so happens that Shara-Rose's assignment to me this summer is to try to be more aware of my deepest emotional needs. And I *need* you to come back to work at TAG this summer."

"Sorry," I repeat. "I've got the summer off."

"Don't be ridiculous, Babette. TAG won't be waiting for you in September if you don't help me now."

I look pointedly at my watch. "You're already five minutes late for your appointment with Shara-Rose, and she's charging you for each minute you stand here harassing me."

"I won't have a cent to my name anyway once TAG closes its doors for good," he mutters. "You really are heartless, Babette. Just because George is a successful lawyer, you're not worried about paying your rent. But I am. Remember your roots! You were once just a lower-middle-class kid from the Bronx!"

I gather all my strength and pull him out of the elevator doorway. Luckily, he's not much bigger than I am. I get in fast and ring for the lobby.

"Don't you care about the future of American theater, about the future of world theater?" he shouts at me as the door closes. "And don't you care whether Alex gets to make her debut at TAG?"

During the elevator ride down, I breathe deeply and reassure myself that Jay is wrong, and that I'm a terrific arts administrator and that I *do* care, passionately, about original theater, and that I'm a wonderful aunt and that the last thing a six-year-old girl really needs is a gig at TAG, and that, no matter what happens, even if George tells me that he's madly in love with Nicole Burden and our marriage ends, I'd be able to find another job, despite the fact that arts administration isn't exactly a booming field during these tough times, and that really, in every way, I'd be just fine on my own.

The elevator lands in the lobby, and I hold the door open for an elderly woman with brightly hennaed hair, carrying a Siamese cat in her arms. "Thank you," she says, shuffling slowly into the elevator. "My children are all grown," she informs me as the elevator doors close, "and Nikolai here," she nods at the cat, who's fast asleep, "is all I have left."

I try to give her an encouraging, upbeat smile before I turn away, and I wonder whether I would be better off just spending the rest of my life alone with Flaca, who's never caused a single crisis in my life.

6

Flaca greets me at the door. After so many years together, she and I have a special rapport. Sometimes I believe that she and I can read each other's minds. I kneel down and rub her soft belly. I trust her a lot more than I trust George these days.

The next thing I do, Flaca following slowly at my heels, is check the answering machine in my bedroom. The only message is from Jay. "I'll expect you at TAG around noon," he says authoritatively. He must have called bright and early while I was still battling out the journal-therapy issue with Shara-Rose, before he waylaid me at the elevator. Sighing, I erase his message.

Flaca follows me into the kitchen. I feed her, and then I grind up some coffee beans. When my coffee is ready, I sit down at the kitchen table, with Flaca on my lap. She's so heavy, I have to shift in order to take her weight.

I look up at the plastic pink tulip-shaped clock, a gift from Maya. It's eleven thirty. George, who gets to work at nine, has probably already held at least two urgent meetings with Nicole Burden.

The thought of Nicole and George together emboldens me, so I grab the roll of paper towels hanging over the sink and the chewed-up pencil I use to make shopping lists. Paper towels and a stubby pencil—they'll be what I use for my damned journal, and if Shara-Rose doesn't like it, well, that's too bad. I refuse to go to some over-priced stationery store and buy a fabric-covered book with a coy little lock and "My Diary" written in flowery script on the cover.

Although I'm furious at Shara-Rose, I have to admit that she has been on target lots of times. For instance, she's the one who first suggested I take off from TAG this summer, which, for her sake, I'll never let Jay know. I rip a paper towel from the roll.

I feel myself sweating as I begin to write. I bite my lip. I hear myself grinding my teeth. It's a distant sound, out of my control, almost abstract. I begin to write.

Dear Beatle George Harrison, I apologize for not having followed your career much lately, but I did read in a magazine in my gynecologist's waiting room that you've had a recent comeback. Also, that you're married now and have a son.

So, first of all, how did you ever make the momentous decision to have a child? Because the truth is, I'm not a hundred percent sure about motherhood. Even though my biological clock is ticking. Also, I keep thinking—and I'm embarrassed to admit this to you, since you were a Beatle before you were even twenty-five—that I haven't yet achieved my full potential, that there's something I'm destined to do, although I don't know what it is.

I look up at the clock; only five minutes have gone by, although it feels like five hours, and that distant sound of grinding teeth is really getting on my nerves. I force myself to continue.

There's just one more thing, before I call this journal stuff quits for today, whether Shara-Rose likes it or not, because the truth is, writing

_still makes me nervous, and I don't feel one iota closer to having pro-
found insights about anything._

_The last time I saw Nicole Burden—the woman I suspect my hus-
band is involved with—was close to a year ago. I had nothing against
her then. I'd gone to pick George up at work, and she was standing by
the water fountain wearing a fur coat. I couldn't decide whether she was
on her way out, or whether she just likes to keep her fur coat on all day.
She was wearing surprisingly unlawyerlike red pointy shoes with high,
spiked heels, the kind we used to call 'Fuck-Me shoes' back in the
Bronx. So what do you think? Is George sleeping with her or not?_

I finish, feeling exhausted and spent, even from writing such a
short entry. That distant sound of grinding teeth stops. I'm so
sweaty, I'm going to have to change my shirt.

Flaca wakes up, climbs down off my lap, and begins eating again.

The phone above the counter rings. Warily, I pick it up, expecting to hear Jay's voice.

"Babette," a polished female voice says, "it's Nicole Burden."

Flaca stops eating—a minor miracle in itself—and looks up at
me with troubled, sympathetic eyes, as though she understands
that this is the phone call that will undo me forever. Nicole
Burden? Calling me? What's going on here? How many traumas is
a girl supposed to endure in one morning? I'm sweating anew, and
the sound of grinding teeth starts up again, even louder than
before. I hope it doesn't carry over phone wires.

Flaca whimpers softly. Perhaps she's frightened that if this
phone call from Nicole Burden makes me go mad with grief, and if
I spend the rest of my days unemployed and wandering the streets,
nobody will be around to take care of her. And perhaps she's right.
Is there any guarantee that Nicole Burden will let George keep
Flaca in their illicit little love nest?

"Babette, are you there?" The polished voice on the other end
of the line expects an answer.

"Yes, Nicole." I find my voice somewhere, somehow, but my tone is the grim tone of someone awaiting the executioner's blow.

"I was wondering if we could have lunch next week. I'd like to speak to you about something. Would that be possible?"

She's not the granddaughter of Abner Burden for nothing. Abner Burden was ruthless, a kind of lawyer robber baron, a self-made millionaire who probably never gave one dime to the poor. I sense a similar ruthlessness in Nicole. She's going to turn the worst moment of my life into nothing more than a routine business lunch for her. She's going to tell me that she and George are in love, and that she wants me to step aside. Maybe she'll threaten to kill me if I refuse. A woman who practices law in Fuck-Me shoes is capable of anything.

She doesn't wait for my reply. "Next Wednesday at noon," she says, naming a restaurant on my block, one I've passed a thousand times but haven't gone into because it looks so pretentious.

I don't need to write it down. There's no way I'll forget the time and place of my own execution. I hang up. "Nicole Burden," I whisper to Flaca, "is my burden to bear." Neither Flaca nor I smile at my sad little attempt to be flip. Instead, Flaca commits a truly selfless act: She leaves her food and climbs back onto my lap. I stroke her warm, familiar fur, determined that no matter what Nicole Burden tells me next Wednesday, and no matter what happens, Flaca and I will never be separated.

7

Shara-Rose is wearing gray sweatpants and a gray sweatshirt, and she's sitting in a full lotus position on her rug. "Read your journal entry to me," she says.

It's unnerving me to have to look down at her, so I slide down from the armchair and sit across from her on the rug. "It was excruciating enough writing it," I explain, arranging my body into my own halfhearted version of a lotus position, "without having to read it out loud to you." She's really getting on my nerves.

Still in perfect lotus position, she pulls a small compact from the pocket of her gray sweatpants and checks her lipstick, which is bright orange. She licks a few specks of lipstick off her teeth, and then she grins at me. Her grin strikes me as wicked. She still has some lipstick on her teeth. Ordinarily I would tell her, but because she's getting on my nerves so much, I decide that it will serve her right to spend the rest of the day with orange teeth.

She lights a cigarette and starts puffing away.

"Why do you bother studying yoga and trying to be healthy," I ask, "if you're going to smoke?"

"I'll have to be sure to ask *my* therapist that," she snaps. "But what I'm asking *you* to do is to read your journal entry to me."

"Here, why don't you just read it yourself?" I slide the paper towels toward her.

"I hope you used a good brand," Shara-Rose says, not cracking a smile. "An absorbent one."

Ignoring her, I rise stiffly from my quasi-lotus position. I reach for *The Kama Sutra*, the ancient Hindu love manual, which is sitting in her bookcase next to *Beyond the Pleasure Principle* by Freud. I settle back down on the rug, and, while she reads my paper towel letter to Beatle George, I read *The Kama Sutra*. I learn that, depending on the depth of her *yoni*, a woman is considered either a deer, a mare, or an elephant.

Shara-Rose looks up from the towels. She blows smoke from the corner of her mouth. "Why do you care so much about Nicole Burden's shoes?"

I shrug, refusing to allow her to bait me.

Shara-Rose stubs out her unfinished cigarette and lights another. "You know, Babette, if you would just stop resisting me, we could try to understand your journal together, so that maybe before your lunch date with Nicole Burden—which, by the way, is only a few days away—we could figure out what's stopping you from just saying, 'Hey, George, are you screwing that blond snot-nose in her Fuck-Me shoes or what?' It's just not like you not to be direct with him. You may not be as aggressive as, say, Arnold Schwarzenegger, but you're not a shrinking violet, either."

I shrug again and continue to read *The Kama Sutra*. "Did you know," I ask, not looking up at her, "that men are either hares, bulls, or horses, depending on the size of their *lingams?*"

"I'm pleased that you're so fascinated by *lingams*, but this is getting us nowhere. Can you manage to let down your witty little defenses for five minutes? This isn't amateur night at The Improv, you know."

I look up at her. She's rocking slightly from side to side in her lotus position, which I assume means she's excited. If I aim very carefully and fling _The Kama Sutra_ right at her head, maybe I can decapitate her. New York City would never notice the loss of one psychotherapist. "Shara-Rose, give me a break, will you?" Suddenly—"volatile patient" that I am—I'm near tears.

There's a long silence. "Okay," she says. Her voice is gentle. She leans forward and hands me a tissue, even though I'm not crying. Her gesture seems genuine, and I'm so touched that despite myself, I do let loose and begin to cry.

She speaks softly, watching as my tears fall and my nose runs. "Married men, even intelligent, tender, basically good men who used to gaze up at the stars on their Iowa farms, have been known to cheat. Even men with quite desirable-looking wives who've actually managed to remain monogamous themselves, despite their own wild pasts and despite the many offers they've received over the years from the various _very_ tempting actors, writers, and directors at TAG—and I know all about the offers, Babette, believe me, because you've told me about every single one. And I know that you've worked very hard to maintain your integrity, and I admire you for it. I honestly do." She rises so smoothly and effortlessly from her lotus position that, even through my tears, I'm impressed, and she comes and sits next to me. She puts her arm around me, and I begin to weep on her shoulder.

"I'll confront him today," I mumble. "I will."

We remain this way until our time is up. I stand, blow my nose, and she walks me to the elevator. "Did I hear you say something about confronting him later today?" she asks.

I ring for the elevator. I clear my throat. "Well, I might as well wait until after my lunch with Nicole Burden. I mean, why rush?"

"Oh, come on, Babette, just do it," she urges.

The elevator arrives, and warily I step inside, expecting to be pounced on by Jay, but, to my relief, the elevator is empty.

8

"Cute," George says on the morning of the day I'm to meet Nicole Burden for lunch, pointing at my brand-new lacy black panties.

George is getting ready for work, standing at his bureau, watching me in the mirror as he struggles to knot his tie. I watch him struggle unsuccessfully—he says that farm life never gave him enough experience in knotting ties—and I keep waiting for some sign, like a twitch or an excessive amount of perspiration dripping down his face, revealing that he's in on the plot with Nicole Burden, that he knows that today is the day his lover is about to reveal the truth to his wife. But he's not twitching or perspiring, and there's been no sign yet.

I slip on my bra, also black, lacy, and brand-new. And then I slip on my favorite skirt, also black. Opening my closet, I search for the right blouse to wear. For once, one of Maya's gifts seems perfect: a hyperfeminine, pink silk, ruffled number. As I'm buttoning the blouse and tucking it into the skirt, I ask, "Are you working late tonight?" I try to keep my voice light and easy. And then I see it on his face, the sign I've been waiting for: what all those novelists must mean by "a pained look."

"I don't know," he answers, after the look has passed, and he knots his tie badly one more time, and then unknots it, "how late I'll be tonight. I'll call you later."

"Fine." But the pained look has convinced me that he does, indeed, know about my lunch date. I feel enraged: He knows and yet he's just letting me go ahead and meet her, casually feeding me to the lions. I'm also enraged because I'm sick and tired of studying him for clues. As the suspicious wife, I study his features, his gestures, his words, and especially his silences, for hints of betrayal and guilt. I can remember once, myself, being watched like this—the year that I'd promised fidelity to Frank, a chiropractor and my "official" boyfriend at the time, and somehow found myself also sleeping with Robert, Frank's best buddy since childhood, who also was a chiropractor. I hadn't meant to hurt either of them, of course. It just happened. But I remember both of them watching me in just this same way, searching for signs of the betrayal they each sensed in me.

"You're getting dressed up," George says.

I nod. I wait for him to say, "Oh, don't bother. Nicole won't pay any attention to your clothes, anyway."

Instead, he looks at me with curiosity. "Why? Do you have plans?"

I change my mind; now I'm convinced he doesn't have the slightest idea about my lunch with Nicole Burden. The pained look probably just meant that he'd knotted his tie too tightly. This lunch date must be Nicole's idea alone. It's she, the ambitious mistress, who must want to lay her cards on the table, while George, the deceitful husband, would probably happily shuttle back and forth between wife and mistress forever. And why not? He's got the best of both worlds. I watch him unknotting his damned tie yet again and I hate him. I really do.

But an instant later, just as he finally knots his tie perfectly, an unexpected feeling of tenderness comes over me and I don't hate him at all. In fact, I want to kiss him. At a moment like this, such a desire on my part must be pure masochism. Nevertheless, unable to resist, I walk over to him. Instead of kissing him, I bite him on the neck, wishing I were a vampire so that from now on he would have to do my bidding. Together, a vampire husband-and-wife team, we'd make love endlessly through the centuries. Maybe we'd even give birth to a vampire baby or two. I bite him a second time, and a third, and each bite becomes more impassioned, more vampirish.

"Come to bed," I say.

I watch him hesitate. Why should he get undressed all over again—after all, he's finally knotted his tie perfectly—just to make love to me? What's the urgency, the rush? Why be late for work, when I'll be there later on, anyway? And it's true: A wife, unlike a mistress, is always there.

But he does get undressed and he comes to bed. He bites me on my neck equally passionately. As soon as he does, however, I begin to withdraw from him, because suddenly I picture him kissing her, and I wonder if, as he's kissing me, he's really thinking of her, and then I imagine the two of them as the eternally bound vampires, together plotting my destruction. "Babette," he moans, lying on top of me, and his voice sounds so loving that I shake off the images and give myself to him fully. It is me that he loves, only me, and I give him my full attention, and he slides my skirt up around my waist and he pulls my black lace panties off, and we make love. Half-dressed like this, I feel excited and vaguely decadent, more like a mistress than a wife. I also feel a twinge of envy for Nicole Burden, who must have the pleasure of feeling like this a lot these days. We lie back. I'm exhausted, but also filled with energy. I glance at the clock. It's 9:25. He'll be about an hour late for work.

He sits on the edge of the bed. He's silent for a long moment. "I *do* love you," he says, finally.

And that's when I know, conclusively, that he really is sleeping with her. It's his emphasis on the word _do_ that gives him away. It's the emphasis of a guilty man. A man who, perhaps, sometimes thinks _do not_ instead of _do_, a man who, in fact, also may be saying the same exact words to someone else.

So, I have to ask myself—as I agonize over that emphasized, giveaway _do_-word—why, of all people, is he cheating on me with _her_? I turn over and lie on my stomach, as I try to figure it out: Why Nicole Burden? Well, it doesn't take me long to come up with an answer. I know exactly what her allure is. She's a blue blood, an Ice Queen. She's the opposite of me, the hot-blooded Bronx-born girl. Maybe, once upon a time, I had seemed exotic to him, in those early days when he'd first arrived in New York from Sioux City, but clearly, no longer. By now he must know that we Bronx girls are a dime a dozen, bred like rabbits by our own hot-blooded Jewish parents back during the postwar Baby Boomer years. True, it was my very hot-blooded aggressiveness in bed that had—as I'd expected and hoped—won him over on our very first night together, even inspiring him to tell me that very night that he'd also fallen in love with me on the spot, in Armstrong's.

But now, I figure, he's used to me. Now he probably feels that I've emasculated him with all my sexual knowledge, the wimpy bastard! Most men would _kill_ to have a woman as uninhibited, passionate, and playful in bed as I, a woman unafraid to walk boldly into The Pleasure Chest and to purchase, without so much as a blush, whatever sex toys might strike her fancy that day, and then actually to go ahead and _use_ them!

I turn over onto my back again and glance once more at the clock. George, who's been stroking my back, oblivious to the rage within me, will soon rise from the bed, get dressed again, knot his tie badly one more time, and then head off for yet another day of fun and games at the office, fun and games most definitely not involving toys from The Pleasure Chest, since it's impossible to imagine Nicole—the Ice Queen—ever setting foot within a sex emporium, let alone knowing what any of the toys were supposed to be *for*, in the first place.

What I want to do now, even though he and I have just made love, and even though he's just declared his love for me, is to murder him. Instead, I do something easier: I close my eyes, so that I can pretend that it's Beatle George to whom I've just made love, instead of my own deceitful George. Maybe it is "groupie-ish," but the way I see it, whatever works, works!

At the same time, in the midst of my fantasizing about Beatle George, I also make a momentous decision: If it turns out that I'm right, and if he is, in fact, sleeping with her—no, I amend that— *when* I discover for a fact that he is, I shall *never, never* speak to him again! Never. That will be my revenge. I'll show him that an aggressive, hot-blooded girl from the Bronx can have ice water running through *her* veins, too. Although I will *not* wear Fuck-Me shoes. That far I will not go, to play my part, since one thing I did learn from having had two chiropractor boyfriends in my past is that eventually all those women in their supposedly sexy Fuck-Me shoes end up needing foot surgery for pinched toes, bunions, and swaying backs. Me, I'll stick with my lace-up, black boots with the comfortable rubber soles, my sneakers, and—my very favorites— my black shimmery flats with the red rhinestones and metal studs all over them, half fairy-tale shoes, half avant-garde. Once upon a time, shortly after the night of our first lovemaking—a few weeks later, after a similarly uninhibited, passionate evening—George had gone so far as to compliment me, unprompted, on my taste in shoes. "You wear the cutest shoes," he'd said, as we lay naked in bed together. "But they're not *just* cute," he continued, staring at my black boots, which had been flung carelessly across the room, "they're also really sensual—really *hot*—just like you, Babette. Your shoes," he'd declared, emphatically, in his soft-spoken way, as though he were having an incredible epiphany, "are like a a *metaphor* for exactly who you are." I remember sighing with happiness, thinking how wonderful it was to love a man who didn't expect me to try to become like some Playboy Centerfold, hobbling around in Fuck-Me shoes.

Well, clearly, his taste in shoes, metaphors, and women has changed a lot since then. Just remembering all this makes me feel even more enraged, as I continue to lie still in bed. He's betrayed my bunion-free feet, my shoes, and ultimately, _everything about_ me, my very "Essence of Babette," in a way. Well, he'll be sorry. If I really set my mind to it, I can do it: never, never speak to him again.

I've already had some heavy-duty practice in dishing out the cold, silent treatment. I'm no novice, as George will soon discover. When Maya and I were in high school, she did something so heinous to me that I didn't speak to her for six months, _not a single word_, and not even my parents could change my mind. What had Maya done? She had stolen my boyfriend at the time, Ricky. I adored Ricky. I thought he looked just like Peter Noone of Herman's Hermits, not exactly _the_ greatest heartthrob of my life, not Beatle George, but not bad at all. Ricky, like Maya, was a senior. I was a junior. But he wasn't her type at all. She didn't like boys with long hair and slightly crooked front teeth, whereas I adored them—and still do. Yet one day she appeared at our dinner table, wearing his ring. And, at the same time, he began turning his head and ignoring me when he passed me in the school corridors.

"But I _didn't steal_ him from you, Babette," she'd kept insisting to me, after I'd informed her that I would never speak to her again. "He's a _person_. He can't be 'stolen.' He's not like those empire-waist dresses I shoplifted those times in Alexander's because I didn't have my allowance money with me. Babette, he _came_ to me voluntarily. He called me and asked me out. He'd already stopped calling you, anyway. He hadn't called you for two whole weeks. Anybody but you would have figured it out, but you're so conceited, you probably thought he just needed a little break from your _intense_ personality, right?"

She *was* right, although I didn't let on. I hadn't been able to believe that a boy with whom I'd been making out passionately for months—I was still a virgin then—and who looked just like sweet Peter Noone of Herman's Hermit's, would just dump me without the courtesy of at least telling me he was doing so! And the weirdest thing was, as soon as he began dating Maya, he cut his long hair very short and began wearing braces to fix his crooked, toothy grin, so that he no longer even looked a thing like Peter Noone.

"Okay, I forgive you for not speaking to me, Babette, for six whole months," Maya had said magnanimously to me, when I finally did deign to speak to her again. "I've decided, though, that you're a little bit crazy sometimes, and that you can't help yourself. I even spoke to the school psychologist about you, and she agreed. She said that some people hold grudges like mad, and simply don't know how to forgive and forget, like normal people." "Well," I'd answered, equally magnanimously, "*some* people might find it a 'little bit crazy' for a sister to start dating her sister's boyfriend after only two weeks, but I forgive you, too." I also didn't believe a word she'd said about the school psychologist, since I knew for a fact that our Bronx public school couldn't *afford* to hire one, and that the last time a psychologist had visited that school was when I was still a sophomore, and I'd been sent to her to try analyze why my term papers were always so late. She'd told me to keep a neat looseleaf notebook, and to be sure to do my homework without the TV on, and that was all.

And the only reason I'd even begun speaking to Maya at all after six months was because Ricky had done exactly the same thing to her. He hadn't called her for two weeks—and, just like me, she had chosen to ignore this sign—and then one day he'd appeared at school holding hands with another girl, a blond airhead whose family had just moved to the Bronx from Venice Beach, California, which had made her seem very exotic to the rest of us, even if her nickname was the dumb-sounding "Cup-

cake." And for Cupcake, Ricky had given himself a whole other
"look": a Bronx surfer-boy look, if such a thing was possible, which
didn't appeal to me, or to Maya, either. "That weasel," Maya and I
had agreed—a very rare occasion, the two of us agreeing on anything, let alone a male.

So as I lie here in bed, listening to George getting ready a second time to head over to his office, remembering how cold and
silent I'd been to Maya during those six months, I know that I've
got what it takes to do it again. And, I decide, in addition to not
speaking to him, I'll find other ways to revenge myself upon him:
If he _asks_ me for a divorce, I won't let him have it; and if he _doesn't_
want a divorce, I'll insist upon having one. Maya and her "invented" school psychologist may have been right, after all—maybe I
am "a little bit crazy." But what is it they say? Hell hath no fury
like one of us scorned? Well, I'll show George just how true that
old phrase can be, how it can be reinterpreted to fit the times,
even times like ours, when betrayal and adultery aren't taken as
seriously as they once were, except, it seems, by me.

9

The restaurant is a block and a half from my apartment. I arrive exactly on time, but Nicole already is seated by the window, ignoring the basket of hot bread in the center of the table.

"Babette, thank you for coming." Her tone is formal, and she isn't smiling as she greets me.

"My pleasure," I lie, attempting to be equally formal. I'm unable to meet her gaze. I sit across from her and stare out the window, meeting the gaze, instead, of a woman who's standing outside staring in at us. I've seen her many times on 57th Street. Usually, she sits alone on a bench in the small, abandoned plaza on the corner of Ninth Avenue where many homeless people live, right in the shadow of one of the most expensive buildings on the block. Today she's carrying one huge shopping bag in each hand. One shopping bag is filled with empty soda bottles and the other with what looks like rags. She stares grimly at me. Guiltily, I turn away from her, but I'm still unable to meet Nicole's gaze. I look around the restaurant, which isn't crowded yet. By twelve thirty, I suspect, it will be jammed with the business lunch crowd.

A waitress comes over. Her long platinum blond hair falls to her waist, and she's wearing a skimpy halter top, a silver miniskirt, and a pair of false eyelashes, letting us know, of course, that she's an actress between parts. "Ladies," she bats the false eyelashes at Nicole, "will you be having anything to drink?"

Nicole orders a mineral water with lime. She must want to be as cool and sober as possible during our tête-à-tête. I suspect that she's also a vigilant calorie watcher.

I have a very different agenda. I'd like to get as drunk as possible, and I don't care if I gain twenty pounds doing it. "A vodka martini, straight," I order boldly. I'm not a drinker, and I've heard that vodka martinis are particularly potent. If a life of loneliness is about to begin for me here in this restaurant with Nicole Burden's imminent announcement, then it might as well begin with a bang. And Nicole must be pleased; if I'm really a lush, then she's simply doing a good deed by rescuing George from me.

The waitress brings our drinks. I take a long, long sip of the martini. My lacy black bra is starting to ride up, but I resist tugging at it because Nicole is staring right at me.

"You look well," she says, sizing me up and sounding completely insincere, as though she has X-ray vision and knows that my bra won't stay put.

I refuse to respond in kind, although, of course, she looks extremely good. Her blond hair is combed into soft waves, she's wearing a strand of real pearls around her neck and an elegantly tailored beige linen suit. But I can't resist: I have to know whether she's wearing her Fuck-Me shoes. The martini must be taking effect. Very deliberately, and, I hope, very subtly, I knock my napkin to the floor. Bending down to retrieve it, I take a peek and can hardly believe my eyes. There they are—the pointy, red spike-heeled Fuck-Me shoes.

I sit up. The waitress is back. "May I take your orders now, ladies?" she simpers, looking at Nicole. Perhaps she's hoping that Nicole will bankroll a Broadway show for her to star in. "Certainly," Nicole says, staring at me, not even giving the waitress a glance, "the sole."

"The sole," I repeat, knowing that there's no point in my bothering to look at the menu, since the martini is absolutely, definitely, positively having an effect, and I wouldn't be able to focus on the small print describing the difference between Chicken Meuniére and Chicken Cacciatore.

I sip moodily at my martini. Nicole doesn't say a thing. I'll be damned if I'm going to chitchat just to help her feel at ease. "You and George certainly seem to have your hands full at work these days," I mutter.

She nods coolly. She sips her mineral water. "Your hairstyle is quite becoming."

She hasn't taken my bait. Clearly, she prefers to make small talk about my Veronica Lake do, before coming in for the kill. I don't reply, and we sit in silence until the waitress brings us our lunch: two slim slices of gray-colored sole on each plate, with slivers of overcooked zucchini on the side. She bats her eyes, but Nicole still seems to have eyes only for me.

I dig in. The sole is hot and tender. I may be about to lose a husband, but I'm hungry anyway. Nicole, though, doesn't even lift her fork. She just takes another dainty sip of her mineral water.

"Martinis go well with sole," I lean forward intimately, "but the zucchini is terribly overcooked." I'm very fuzzy-headed, and I have a strong urge to see her shoes again. A lot less subtly, I drop my napkin a second time, and I bend down and stare underneath the table at her shoes. When I bring my head up I accidentally bang it on the table. "Ouch," I say, "I just love your shoes, Nicole. Where did you find them?" I gulp down what's left of my martini. I call the waitress over and order another.

"You certainly like martinis," Nicole says, coolly.

"Love them," I declare, slurping my second one loudly.

"And," she says, moving her sole around on her plate with her fork, "how is TAG doing these days?"

Tipsy or not, I'm in awe. This woman, my husband's lover, must truly be the Queen of Small Talk. I guess she inherited the ability from ancestors who had to make a lot of it during the May-flower voyage.

"TAG," I tell her, trying not to slur my words, "is fine. Truly exquisite." I like the sound of that. "Truly exquisite," I repeat. Why tell her that TAG is about to become like the homeless woman who's back outside our window, staring in at us.

"I have a cousin...." Nicole says. Her voice trails off. I must be so drunk that I'm having aural hallucinations. Why, at a time like this, would she want to tell me about a cousin? She must have said, "I have a confession." Or maybe, "I have your husband." I try to concentrate.

"My cousin's name is Sarah," she goes on, "and she's just gradu-ated from Sarah Lawrence."

What does Sarah from Sarah Lawrence have to do with any-thing? Are Nicole and George involved in some sort of quasi-inces-tuous ménage à trois with a college girl?

"Sarah adores the arts. She wants to go into arts administration."

I'm nearly finished with my second martini. When will Nicole Burden stop making small talk about her relatives and get to the point?

"And I was wondering," Nicole says, with a phony smile, "wheth-er Sarah could help out at TAG, on a voluntary basis, of course, just for the experience."

I'm dumbfounded. This goes beyond banal small talk; this is insidious and evil.

"I'm sure you must be understaffed at TAG these days," she continues. "The arts are hardly thriving in this economy, as you undoubtedly know firsthand. And Sarah does love to write. Per-haps you need someone to help out with correspondence, grant proposals, things like that."

She's not asking me whether I'd like someone to help me do the writing. She's *telling* me. I have a strong suspicion that George must have betrayed me even further by informing her about my writing anxiety. Or is she some sort of witch with intuitive powers? Maybe her ancestors settled in Salem when they came over.

I begin to laugh. "Sure, Nicole. Tell your cousin Sarah to call Jay Adroit at TAG any time." I keep laughing.

"Thanks so much," she says, looking decisively at her watch. "Babette, I'm sorry, but I've got to rush off to a meeting. I'm afraid I'm late already." She signals the waitress for the check.

"Really, do have Sarah call Jay." I'm still laughing. "TAG is such a truly, truly exquisite place to work."

"I will," she says. "And there's no need for you to leave just because I've got to run off. You stay and finish your martini."

"Sure." I tug at my bra.

"A lovely blouse," Nicole says, watching me tug away. She puts the bill on her credit card. "Pink becomes you." She rises and shakes my hand, which I'm having trouble holding steady. And then she's gone, poof, vanished, out the door of the restaurant. Through the window, I watch her walk past the homeless woman, to the curb, where a taxi arrives on command, as though it's her personal limo.

"A doggie bag," I tell the waitress, who's hovering around the table. I point to Nicole's untouched sole, my untouched zucchini slices, and the leftover bread. The waitress clears the table and returns a few minutes later with two containers and some bread wrapped in aluminum foil.

I leave the restaurant and hand the food to the woman standing outside. She thanks me, and places it carefully in one of her shopping bags. I hope she doesn't mind overcooked zucchini and lukewarm sole.

I begin to navigate the short journey home. I'm not so drunk that I don't understand that Shara-Rose was right. Now I must confront George directly, after all, just like the doctor ordered.

10

Flaca meets me at the door. Her expression is quizzical, as though she knows I'm drunk. When I bend down to pet her, my head starts pounding.

She follows me to the bedroom, where I intend to collapse into a deep sleep. But first I have to turn down the volume on the answering machine so that I can shield myself from Jay's calls. I'm definitely not in the mood to be woken up by his latest woes about Acme Developers.

I climb into bed, not bothering to get undressed. My head is still pounding, and when I close my eyes, the room spins even harder. I'm determined to will myself to sleep, so that when I awaken, I'll be completely sober. As sober as Nicole Burden. I wake up a couple of hours later. Flaca is draped across my knees. My throat is dry. My bra is completely twisted, up somewhere around my neck. There's a big run in my pantyhose, as though I clawed my leg in my sleep. The worst part is that the room is still spinning.

I glance over at the answering machine. The red light is blinking. With difficulty, I try to rise. Flaca takes her time undraping herself from my knees.

I force myself to stand, and I walk over to the answering machine. I press the Play button. Jay sounds extremely excited: "Babette, some Sandy Burden person called, or maybe it's Susie Burden, anyway, she's coming by the office tomorrow! I want you to come by, too, to meet her."

So Nicole wasted no time letting her little cousin Sarah know about TAG. And Sarah is no procrastinator, either. After I erase Jay's message, I carry the phone back to bed. I dial George's number at Burden, Lawrence, Shapiro, and O'Reilly.

Sheila, the secretary, answers. "Mr. Harrison's line," she says, in her typically affectless tone.

"It's desperately urgent, Sheila," I say, "please get George."

"Will *do!*" she responds, sounding more animated than I've ever heard her. She must be one of those people who thrives on crises, especially other people's crises.

A moment later George gets on. "What's wrong?"

"Come home." My voice sounds spooky.

"Why? What's wrong?"

Oh, to have a husband who didn't ask questions, who just jumped on command. "Just do it, George. I mean it." I hang up.

The room is spinning a lot less now. To my surprise, I decide that I liked it better when it was spinning ferociously. I walk to the living room where we keep a full bar in the oak cabinet above the stereo. George doesn't drink much either, but he says that New York City lawyers are required to keep full bars, that it's part of their job.

I open the cabinet doors and stare at the various bottles, realizing that I haven't the vaguest idea what goes into a vodka martini besides vodka. I decide to have my vodka straight. Three straight shots of it one after another. Flaca is sitting on the sofa across the room watching me. She looks less quizzical now, and more worried.

The room is spinning wildly again, tumbling around and doing somersaults, just the way I like it. I have a sudden urge to hear the old Blood, Sweat and Tears song "Spinning Wheel." I bend down and on my knees I begin going through our huge stack of old albums. It feels good to fling record albums around the room. Maybe I'm really a performance artist, like Lydia Smart, and I'm taking on the persona of a wild, drunken woman whose heart is breaking. Maybe I can perform it at TAG one day. I wish Lydia were here in the room to see me. She'd be proud.

Finally, I find the Blood, Sweat and Tears album. I attempt to rise from the floor with dignity, so that Flaca will stop looking so worried. I attempt to place the album on the turntable—wishing I had the song on CD, which would be a lot easier to maneuver, because right now putting the album down where it belongs seems to require far more eye-and-hand coordination than I possess. After much struggling, I manage to get the album to settle down, and I turn around and bow at Flaca.

I attempt to sing along, knowing I'm getting the words all wrong. I make my way across the room to join Flaca on the sofa. But she moves, rather quickly for her, toward the far end of the sofa. I continue to sing my own lyrics, which, I'm fairly certain, bear no resemblance to the song's.

A few minutes later, or maybe it's a few hours later or a few years later, George comes in. His tie is crooked and his hair is mussed. I've lost my sense of time. Maybe I've gone completely gray waiting for him; maybe Flaca is now a thousand years old.

My eyes feel as though they're crossing against my will, and I see two of him. And then three.

"What's wrong?" George asks, looking at me with a horrified expression. Could I have DTs already? Am I on the road to Skid Row this quickly? Because I'm definitely seeing three horrified-looking Georges. I see the three of them taking it all in: the scattered record albums, the nervous cat, the bottle of vodka, the drunken wife. "What are you doing?" they all ask me. I feel hot. Very hot. I look at the three Georges through heavily lidded eyes. I enunciate carefully, determined not to slur my words. I'm enunciating so carefully, in fact, that I'm bordering on sounding British. "I'm not doing anything, George. Really. I'm feeling truly exquisite," I lie. "Truly exquisite. But there is something that I wish to discuss with you." And with *you* and *you*, I add silently to the two other Georges. "George," I continue, and *George* and *George*, I add silently again, and I cross my legs for emphasis, although I start to dip over too much to one side and I have to right myself, "are you sleeping with Nicole Burden?" There. I've said it. Loud and clear. I wish Shara-Rose were here in the room to have heard me being so direct and assertive. Arnold Schwarzenegger, move over.

"Babette," one of the three Georges answers, his expression pained, and again I can't tell if he's answered me immediately or whether hours or years have passed since I asked my question, "no, I'm not. But yes, I was."

The Blood, Sweat and Tears album is still playing, but now I can't make out any of their words, and George keeps talking but I can't make out any more of his words, either. The three Georges compress into one George, and every time he says something, the words go right from his mouth into a bubble, and the bubble hangs in the air over his head, like a comic-book bubble. But none of the letters in the bubbles over George's head are clear. They're all fuzzy and unreadable. I've lost not only my husband, but the ability to hear and speak, to use language. It's a terrible feeling. Being drunk isn't at all fun.

I take a deep breath. I feel desperate to regain the use of my voice. "Bye-bye," I hear myself whispering, although I'm saying it to myself, not to George. And now I know exactly what I'm going to do, at least for the moment. And, after all the vodka I've had, it's easy enough to accomplish. I smile slightly as I pass out on the sofa.

11

Debbie, the Quickie-Weight-Loss instructor, is standing in the front of the large, high-ceilinged, gymnasiumlike room, which is decorated with large plastic replicas of human fat cells. She's instructing Maya, me, thirty other women in various shapes and sizes, and two men, on how to diet. Debbie was Maya's assistant at Pretty in Pink before she lost fifty pounds and began spreading the word of the Quickie-Weight-Loss Program.

Maya insisted that I come to this meeting with her, after I called her yesterday to tell her that I'd left George and wasn't speaking to him. I also made the whopping mistake of mentioning that I'd gained five pounds in the mere seven days since he told me about Nicole Burden, and since I moved out.

"At that rate," Maya had said, "in a year you'll weigh about four hundred pounds."

"Fine," I answered, "and then I'll die of a heart attack and George and Nicole Burden can have that on their consciences, too."

"Always my kid sister," she snapped, and from someone else, the words might have sounded affectionate. "I expect to see you tomorrow at Debbie's eleven o'clock class."

Maya doesn't need to diet either, but about twice a year she panics, convinced that she's gaining weight, and that her clients are all going to dump her for a slimmer designer.

Debbie is speaking enthusiastically to the group. I try to concentrate on what she's saying, but I've been walking around in a fog, having trouble concentrating on anything for the last seven days. Jay keeps calling with TAG news, the latest being details about the demonstration that the wunderkind Sarah Burden is already busy organizing, but I have trouble even remembering what TAG is.

I stare intently at Debbie, squinting to put her into focus. She's wearing a dignified brown-and-white pinstriped suit, quite different from the hot pink dresses she used to wear during her Pretty in Pink days. "Why have *one* slice of white bread," she asks us with great fervor, "when you can have *two* rice cakes?" Maya pokes me in the ribs. "You really are a little bit crazy, Babette, just like I always said back in high school," she stage whispers, writing down the words *rice cakes* in the margin of her Quickie-Weight-Loss booklet, "to leave George just like that. I mean, he told you it's all over with this other woman. How could you just move out on him the very next morning?"

Debbie is attempting to establish eye contact with Maya, I assume to let Maya know that her voice is carrying, and that everyone in the room now knows that I've just left my philandering husband. Maya doesn't even look up at Debbie. "How could you?" she stage whispers to me again. "So he had a fling. Big deal."

Debbie valiantly continues, trying to ignore the little drama being played out in the middle of the room. "*Two* rice cakes," Debbie says, "with diet jam!"

I shrug. I have no desire to hear any more of Maya's opinions about my decision to leave George, or to stop speaking to him. If I tell her how I really feel, deep down, about my being the hot-blooded Jewish girl without a lot of money to her name, who's been rejected for a blue blood, an Ice Queen, she'll go bananas right here in the midst of all these nearly life-size fat cell replicas, and she'll tell me that I'm not just a _little bit_ crazy, but _very_ crazy, "paranoid and certifiable, I swear," she'll add, "because _nobody_, Babette, thinks of either of us as _Bronx_ girls any longer. That's ancient history. We hardly stick out like kids from the boroughs. You're stuck in the past, on top of everything else!"

The thing is, I don't care what Maya thinks about my theories, or whether she thinks I'm mildly crazy or totally paranoid. Mostly, I feel hurt, wounded, vengeful, confused, and absolutely deter-mined to stick to my guns. After all, I have never, _never_ given in to any of my own urges to sleep with other men since meeting George, and some of those actors at TAG really have come on pretty damned strong. So how dare George give in to _his_ urges? It's really quite simple from a certain perspective. And that Maya doesn't share that perspective doesn't surprise me in the least. After all, she did "steal" my boyfriend back in high school. Not every sister would have said yes when Ricky called to ask her out, even if he _had_ done so "voluntarily." Some sisters might have told him off, in fact, for being a schmuck.

In fact, everyone I knew, including Maya, always had predicted that I'd be the one to cheat once I married George, given my pre-vious track record. Instead, I'd discovered fidelity. And George, who'd never been even slightly wild or promiscuous, who'd had one virginal college girlfriend, one only-slightly-less virginal law school girlfriend, and then me, had ended up being the cheater. And how could I be sure that Nicole Burden was the only one? After all, I knew from personal experience that once you start, it's difficult to stop: For instance, during the period when I was cheat-ing on the two chiropractors—Frank and Robert—there also was

Billy, an unemployed actor with soulful, heavily lashed eyes I'd met on line at a performance art festival. But those days were long past.

So, the bottom line is this: I don't want to sleep beside George again, and I don't want to speak to him. If I do, I'll drive myself absolutely mad looking for hidden meanings, for hints of deception, in every syllable, every pause. The part of him that treasures silence has become loathsome to me. I feel hopeless. Without trust, without communication, there is no more marriage. At least not by my standards, even if those standards may appear to some people to be "a little bit crazy."

Maya pokes me in the ribs again. "Whose apartment did you say you're staying in, anyway?"

Maya is still clearly determined to have her version of a heart-to-heart talk with me—which means, essentially, her giving me advice—in the midst of this Quickie-Weight-Loss meeting.

"I'm staying at Lydia Smart's apartment," I whisper. "She's on tour, and she said that I can stay there as long as I need to. Lydia was *very* understanding." I want Maya to realize that not everyone thinks I'm doing the wrong thing.

"Ssh!" the woman in front of us turns around. Her eyes are beady.

Maya grimaces at the woman, but at least she doesn't poke me in the ribs again.

Debbie begins taking questions from the group. "Yes?" she points to the beady-eyed woman.

"Debbie," the woman speaks intensely, "sometimes when I'm feeling really down, I consume huge amounts of fudge ripple ice cream...."

There's a sympathetic murmur throughout the room. Even in my dazed state, I contribute to it, because I'm certain that in my new life without George, I'm going to have many urges for ice cream—fudge ripple and lots of other flavors. *Let George have his Ice Queen,* I think, *I'll settle for ice cream.*

Maya is poking me again, so that I can't hear Debbie's response. This time, instead of whispering to me at top volume, she hands me a note that she must have written while I was attepting to be inwardly flip about ice cream. It's on her pink business stationery, and it's written in lavender ink, in the same flowery script, with the same three exclamation points, from her girlhood diary. "Don't be a fool, Babette," her note says, "go back to George while he'll still have you!!!"

She hands me her lavender pen. Beneath her flowery note, I scrawl, "How can you, of all people, say such a thing, when your own ex-husband left you because of his affair with that showroom bimbo?" This may not be the most tactful response, but I see no reason for tact.

Maya is busy composing her reply. Her writing pace is fast and furious, and she's concentrating so intently that she's biting down on her bottom lip. Her lipstick matches both her stationery and the flouncy dress she's wearing.

With a wild expression, she hands me her second note. "First of all," this one says, "Merv wasn't merely having an itty-bitty affair, like George is, which is probably over, or at least nearly over, anyway." I wonder whether I should correct her grammar. I decide against it, and continue reading. "Besides, you can't compare yourself to me. We're as different as day and night."

Well, vive la différence, I think. She hands me her lavender pen again. "I'm sorry, but I just can't excuse George's infidelity by quantifying it," I write. I look up at Debbie, who's now giving advice on how to control the urge for fudge ripple ice cream, while Maya is already writing away, replying to my last note. It's clear that Maya doesn't suffer from writing anxiety; Shara-Rose would love her. She hands me her third note.

"Babette," it says, "go back to George, go back and help Jay at TAG, and then have a baby before it's too late!!!" I've never confided in Maya my thoughts about having a baby, so her advice has nothing to do with my needs and desires. She just believes that, when in doubt, women should procreate. I'm so angry I can't even respond. However, I don't feel nearly as much in a daze. Maybe Maya's been good for me, after all.

Debbie is calling the meeting to a close. "Eat healthy," she reminds us, "and eat Quickie-Weight-Loss!"

I glance at my watch. It's noon, and I'm glad the meeting is over.

Maya shakes her head at me as though I'm a lost cause. She slips her notepaper and pen inside her pocketbook.

We ride down the elevator with the beady-eyed woman, who glares at Maya the whole way down. Pointedly ignoring her, Maya looks at me. "Babette," she says, "just do what I told you, okay?"

I ignore her comment. "If you need me, I'll be at Lydia Smart's."

Outside the old office building in which Quickie-Weight-Loss has its offices—undoubtedly one day Acme Developers will want to raze this building to the ground, too—Maya flounces away, off to an appointment with a client who's hired her to redecorate his currently black-and-steel Hamptons summer house completely in pink.

12

The Quickie-Weight-Loss meeting has exhausted me. I sink uncomfortably into one of the ten director's chairs scattered around Lydia Smart's living room. She doesn't seem to believe in sofas. Lydia's apartment is located on 56th and Ninth, which is, as the saying goes, "spitting distance" from my apartment. Or, to be more accurate, the apartment where George now lives alone. And where, according to the phone messages he's been leaving for me every day on Lydia's answering machine, he's consumed by guilt. Yesterday's message was "I promise you that I'll respect your wish to be alone, and that I won't barge in and ravish you."

Lydia was able to buy this two-bedroom apartment because a few years ago she won an Artists for the Arts Fellowship—the first "cutting edge" performer ever to win one. One of the bedrooms is tiny and dark, more like a closet. But the other bedroom is large and airy, with a high ceiling and bright yellow walls. Naturally, I've moved into the tiny, bleak one. It's more appropriate for my mood.

I rouse myself and go into the kitchen, where Lydia keeps her answering machine on the oval wooden kitchen table, next to a Barbie doll dressed in tennis whites and holding a tiny tennis racquet in one raised hand, her body arched and ready to serve.

The first message is from my mother. "Babette," she says happily, "you're welcome to come stay with us for as long as you'd like." But my parents' mood, like Lydia's larger bedroom, is simply too bright and cheerful for me to cope with right now. My parents weren't especially upbeat and chipper when Maya and I were growing up in the Bronx. It must be something in the drinking water in Woodstock.

"Babette," the next message is from Jay, who's starting to sound almost as weary of leaving messages for me as I am of getting them from him, "Sarah and I could really use your help here, you know." Just hearing Sarah's name gives me the creeps. I picture her as a twenty-year-old, penny-loafered version of her cousin Nicole.

Finally, there's today's message from George. One a day, just like a multivitamin. "Babette," he says softly—do I detect a bogus catch in his throat?—"you won't talk to me, but we need to talk. I understand how you feel. Well, maybe I don't." There's a long pause. "Come home. Or at least, meet me for dinner. Talk to me." There's another pause.

Now he wants to talk. But it's a little late. There's no longer a shared language, an Esperanto of our souls. I rearrange Barbie so that she's poised to deliver a mean and violent backhand.

George begins to sing, "I Wanna Hold Your Hand." He's crooning slowly and plaintively, making the Beatles' song into a Bing Crosby number. He must think he's being charming and irresistible. He sings the entire song. I have the most intense urge I've had yet for fudge ripple ice cream. But rather than eating it what I'd like to do is fling it right in his face. I decide to go for a swim at my health club, instead. This will be my first swim in the new era, A.G.—After George.

I walk the block and a half to the club, passing the large group of homeless people on the corner of Ninth, some of whom are sprawled out on the sidewalk, watching a fuzzy picture on an old black-and-white TV, which they've ingeniously connected to the street light in the middle of the block. Seeing them again, I worry that I'll no longer be able to survive in New York on my own. My salary at TAG—_if_ TAG survives—is no great shakes. Arts administrators tend not to earn megabucks, and I'm no exception. Shara-Rose says that her female patients, more than the males, fear homelessness. "You've all got the Bag Lady Blues," she says.

As I make my way, stepping over the sprawled bodies, I give change to a few of them—a quarter here and there—but because there are so many, I have to choose which ones to give to. I'm arbitrary: Some days I'll give only to women. Some days only to elderly men. Today I give only to those women who strike me as looking lovelorn.

Maya, who belongs to one of those prohibitively expensive clubs on the Upper East Side, calls my club "the K-Mart of health clubs." She's referring to the fact that the equipment is old, the ceilings are peeling, the aerobics teachers are chubby, and the female members wear old, stretched-out one-piece bathing suits rather than sexy bikinis. What Maya can't fathom is that these are the very things I like best about the club.

LaDonna, the locker room attendant, who's a single mother from Brooklyn, looks up from the textbook she's studying for her high school equivalency exam. "Hey," she greets me, and then returns to her book.

LaDonna and I always smile and greet each other. But, unlike lots of the women, I don't pour my heart out to her. I've got Shara-Rose for that, and besides, I never feel terribly social in the gym. Today I feel less social than ever. I can still hear George singing "I Wannna Hold Your Hand," formerly one of my favorite Beatles' songs and now ruined for me forever, and I still feel inclined to violence towards him.

I open my locker, which, after only a week away, already seems unfamiliar. I remove my bathing suit, goggles, and bathing cap. The bathing suit, which I bought because it was on sale, is one of the only pink things I've ever voluntarily bought for myself. It's the pink of uncooked fish.

Bravely, I grit my teeth and step into the shower, keeping the water ice cold. Maybe the cold water will dampen my violent urges, the way it supposedly dampens sexual urges in horny men. The woman in the next shower is singing "I Whistle a Happy Tune," from *The King and I*, and I join in softly. But neither the cold shower nor the inspirational song cures me: I'm still furious at George.

Towel, bathing cap, and goggles in hand, I walk down the slippery staircase leading to the pool. Every lane is taken. A number of people are sitting around in beach chairs, clutching numbered tags. Resigned to a long wait, I take a tag down from the hook on the wall.

My number is twelve. Definitely a long wait. I sigh. Not that I've got much else to do. Maybe watching the swimmers going back and forth in their lanes will calm me down, a kind of enforced meditation. I sit in the one empty beach chair, between the afternoon lifeguard, Ari, who's engrossed in doing the *New York Times* crossword puzzle, and another man, about twenty-four, in a skimpy blue-and-white striped bathing suit.

"Crowded," the man in the blue-and-white bathing suit says pleasantly, while I try to relax into a meditative state.

I assume he's talking past me, to Ari. But he's staring at me. His blond hair is pulled back into a short ponytail, and his goggles are hanging around his neck, like a pendant. As attractive as this trim, half-naked man is, however, I'm much too busy nurturing my anger at George—the meditation idea doesn't seem to be working at all—to sit here making banal small talk with him. So I just nod, look down, and become absorbed in playing with my goggles, which, I notice, are scratched.

"You work at TAG," he says.

Surprised, I look up from my goggles.

"I've seen you there a number of times. I'm an actor. I appeared there a couple of years ago in _Early Man_. Do you remember me?"

Although I don't remember him, I definitely remember _Early Man_, a raucous farce about primitive versus contemporary man, with primitive man definitely the winner. _Early Man_ was written and directed by Carlos Carlos, who's one of TAG's playwrights-in-residence. But thinking about _Early Man_ and Carlos Carlos, as I sit here nurturing my anger at George, only makes me angrier, since Carlos Carlos also just happens to be the man with whom Jay's ex-wife was having an affair, and for whom she left Jay. And right now, the thought of any man who lies and cheats doesn't exactly thrill me.

"I was the one in _Early Man_ who invented fire," the man says, interrupting my embittered thoughts about Carlos Carlos and adultery. "My name in the play was Org. But my real name is Trent."

"I'm Babette Bliss." I will myself to banish all thoughts of Carlos Carlos for the moment. I look back down at my goggles. A lane has emptied, and it's Trent's turn. "Listen," he says, "how about if we meet in the lobby in an hour and go out for a beer?"

I wonder whether Trent is sensing my unhappiness. I hope that I'm not sending out "Desperate Single Woman Signals"; I can't stand that stereotyped image of the lonely woman who's hoping for a man, _any_ man. I always turn the TV off when one of those self-deprecating women comics comes on, the ones who say things like, "I was engaged to be married once, but then my fiancé regained his sight...."

Well, maybe this man isn't trying to pick me up. Maybe he's an out-of-work actor hoping that I can get him work at TAG. I look carefully at him: No, he's definitely attracted to me, definitely hoping that after our beer together, we'll move along to a more intimate venue. I feel very flattered by his interest. I also feel quite a bit of bona fide hot lust welling up inside me. And I'm proud of myself for feeling it. After all, why shouldn't I say yes to his offer? Maybe, in fact, we should just forget about the beer altogether and go back to his place immediately. In any case, I nod yes, wondering if my cheeks are turning bright red from the heat in my chest. I look back down at my goggles. He must think I'm obsessed with my goggles.

"Great," he says, "we can go nearby, to Armstrong's."

I feel as though I've just been punched in the stomach. Am I destined to begin my first extramarital affair in the same place in which I met and fell in love with George? I picture the scene: Trent and I are sitting side by side in Armstrong's at the same table at which I met George with Shara-Rose. Trent and I will share a pitcher of beer together, the same way George and I did. And then, as the beer helps us to loosen up, Trent and I will throw our arms around each other and start to kiss passionately. And of course, at that very moment, in will walk George and Nicole Burden. She'll be wearing her Fuck-Me shoes. George will just stand there, looking from me to Trent, and then back to me. He'll be stunned. He'll be miserable. And I'll be happy.

I watch Trent as he sits on the pool edge, adjusting his goggles around his forehead. Even with his goggles on, he looks good, which is saying a lot, since most of the swimmers look like grasshoppers when their goggles are wrapped around their skulls. Before jumping into the water, he turns around and smiles seductively at me. Just as I expect, he's a fast, strong swimmer. His crawl is perfect.

A few minutes later, a lane opens up for me. I also do a very nice crawl, and I can't resist showing it off. Then I switch to a leisurely breast stroke, simply because the name encourages me to be even more sensual in my movements. Finally, after about twenty minutes, I scurry gracefully up the ladder on the side of the pool, and I head back up the stairs.

I take a steamy hot shower this time, and while I shampoo my

hair, I watch a hugely pregnant naked woman arranging her shampoo and conditioner on the bench. I'm impressed that she's still
coming to the gym, considering that she looks as though she very
well could give birth today. With a lovely and mysterious Mona
Lisa smile, she disappears into the corner shower stall, pulling the
faded yellow shower curtain closed.

After I dry off and get dressed, I join the group of about ten
women blow-drying their hair and making up their faces in front
of the mirror. The blow-dryers are arranged in a neat row on a long
table. A few of the women are chatting with each other, compar-
ing the merits of one brand of antichlorine shampoo over another,
as they dry, set, mousse, and spray their hair. But most of them are
quiet, seeming completely absorbed in what they're doing. I look
from one to the other, wondering which ones are happy and
which ones aren't. The pregnant woman, I decide, isn't so happy
after all, despite her earlier Mona Lisa smile. Dressed in a bright
green maternity dress, she applies an unflattering amount of frost-
ed green eyeshadow, thick black mascara, and shockingly red lipstick. There's no Mona Lisa smile on her face now. She fiercely
rubs a bright red gel onto her cheeks, as though she's trying to rub
some happiness in. But it would be presumptuous to think that her
unhappiness is connected to her pregnancy. On the other hand,
who knows? The happiest woman, I suspect, is the one standing by
herself in the corner, applying a creamy lotion to her neck. She's
softly singing "Oklahoma," and I have a hunch that she was the
one in the shower singing "I Whistle a Happy Tune." She looks a
youthful forty. Her auburn hair is long and straight, with bangs,
reminding me of the way the Beatles' mod girlfriends used to wear
their hair.

I want to stay here all day, watching these women, imagining
their lives, which ones are faithful, which ones are unfaithful,
which ones are reconciled to the way things are in their lives, and
which ones—like me—are never reconciled, to anything. Maybe it

will help me to figure out how to live my own life. "Excuse me," I'd like to say to the auburn-haired woman, "have you ever felt *so* betrayed, so deeply hurt by a man that you decided *never* to speak to him again, even if some people seem to find that response 'a little bit crazy?'" I'd also like to ask the pregnant woman why she wears so much tacky makeup and what it feels like when the baby kicks.

But I can't put off my appointment with Trent any longer. I've been blow-drying my hair for so long that my ears are hot. I walk back to my locker, snap shut my combination lock, and say good-bye to LaDonna. She's still reading her textbook, although now she's wearing a Walkman turned up so loud that I can hear the music.

Trent is waiting for me in the lobby, looking patient, sweet, and sexy. He's sitting on the sofa next to the reception desk where Smitty, the black-bearded club manager, is reading a comic book and eating a hero sandwich.

"Babette," Trent greets me, rising. He's wearing the kind of tight T-shirt the boys back in the Bronx wore to show off their muscles, and it looks very good on him.

"Listen," I'm practically whispering in his ear so that Smitty can't hear, "I can't go out with you right now. Even for a beer. I'm married, and I'm in a very strange mood. A *very, very* strange mood." I know my words are making me sound like a combination of highly flirtatious, provocative, and a little crazy, but I can't help myself.

"What kind of 'strange' mood?" Although he looks surprised, he's still giving me a flirtatious, extremely tempting smile.

I don't answer. I just shrug—again, I have a feeling that even though I don't intend it to be, it's a sort of provocative shrug—and then I try to offer my own version of an enigmatic Mona Lisa smile. But what I don't want to do is directly answer his question, to explain that this is the kind of "strange mood" I recognize all too well from my wild single days, the kind of mood that leads me, inevitably, to sex. Within minutes, sometimes. Even these days with all the rules about safe sex, I'd still go ahead and do it—following all the rules, naturally. Trent is a real temptation: I've always had a particularly soft spot for young, beautiful actors, as well as for Herman's Hermits, Beatles, and ex-Beatles. That was one of the reasons I started to work at TAG in the first place—in addition, of course, to my genuine devotion to innovative, cutting-edge theater.

I stare into Trent's eyes, which are clear and luminous, not at all bloodshot after his swim, the way a lot of the swimmers' eyes look afterward, from all the chlorine in the pool. I definitely want to sleep with him—I _feel_ my desire for him so strongly, all through my own body—with his tight T-shirt, and his seductive, pretty boy actor's looks. But alas, it would complicate things too much right now. I might not feel so self-protected, so firm in my belief that I'm entitled to leave George and never to speak to him again. After all, if I start with Trent, then I'm very liable to start calling up some of the other actors from TAG, maybe some of the other ones from _Early Man_, with their terrific, loinclothed, Nautilus-honed bodies. And then what? If I begin having affairs—even if they are only retaliatory—I'll have no _stance_, no justification to feel as hurt as I do. And I really, really _am_ hurting a lot, "a little bit crazy," or not. So I must remain celibate, at least for the time being. Things are growing complicated enough for me without all that other stuff starting. Still, I feel like weeping at the loss of beautiful Trent.

"Well," he smiles, "if you ever get divorced, I'm listed in the phone book. My last name is Johnson."

I'm too startled to respond. How would he know that divorce is very much on my mind these days? "Johnson. I'll be sure to remember."

He waves jauntily and walks out the door.

I linger in the lobby for about five more minutes so that I won't run into him outside. Smitty never looks up from his comic book. I figure he's heard it all before.

This time, as I walk along the block where the homeless people live, I give quarters to a few of the younger men, my way of apologizing to Trent. I'm determined to spend the evening all alone in Lydia's apartment, ignoring the telephone, watching TV with Flaca on my lap.

But I still want to throw ice cream at George, so I make a quick stop at the supermarket. They're all out of fudge ripple; a lot of other women must have been shopping today. I settle for one pint of chocolate chocolate chip and one pint of butter pecan, which seem good enough for eating or flinging in George's face, whichever I decide to do.

13

"So then what?" Shara-Rose asks, after I've recounted yesterday's adventures at the health club to her.

I'm sitting in the black leather armchair, and she's sitting on the black leather sofa, with her chin resting on her knees. She's wearing a V-necked jersey catsuit in a leopard-skin pattern, and, on each wrist, about five plastic bracelets, all painted in a matching leopard-skin pattern.

"I ate the pint of butter pecan for breakfast this morning," I admit, "although I didn't touch the chocolate chocolate chip." Shara-Rose nods briskly, as though this is exactly the answer she expects from such a weak-willed, self-indulgent person. The fact that I resisted the chocolate chocolate chip doesn't seem to impress her. She rises abruptly and begins walking around her office, picking up and discarding empty packs of cigarettes. In her leopard-skin catsuit, she reminds me of a hungry animal scavenging for food. Finally, she finds a pack with a few crushed cigarettes left. Triumphantly, she lights one; it's so old and bent that tobacco flakes are falling out of it like crumbs. She returns to the sofa. For a couple of minutes, she sits quietly, contentedly smoking, looking almost drugged with happiness.

I wait for her to remember that I'm there. Finally, she looks at me as though she's coming out of her drugged state. "Okay," she says, "cough up your latest journal entry."

"There *is* no latest journal entry."

"No latest journal entry? What do you mean?" Shara-Rose violently raises her eyebrows, reminding me of my tenth-grade English teacher, Mrs. Whitehawk. Whenever I didn't turn in a paper on time, Mrs. Whitehawk would raise her thick eyebrows and say, "No term paper, Babette? What do you mean?" And I never had the courage to face those thick eyebrows and say, "Mrs. Whitehawk, the truth is that writing papers makes me anxious and miserable, because I want every word I write, every comma, every period, to be perfect, to be poetry. So I put all this pressure on myself and I make myself crazy because I know I'm bound to fail and then I can't write anything at all." Mrs. Whitehawk wouldn't have been interested. She was much more interested in devising punishments for me, such as writing extra term papers on topics like "Melville's Use of Rhythmic Patterns in the Sentence Struc-ture in the Whaling Chapters of *Moby Dick*." I look at Shara-Rose with the same kind of half-guilty, half-snotty expression with which I used to look at Mrs. Whitehawk.

As fast as lightning, Shara-Rose's expression changes once again. She's very professional, very shrinklike, nothing like Mrs. Whitehawk. "Babette, perhaps you would care, instead, to share some of your recent *feelings* about keeping a journal." Her face is a study in calm, as though she's just achieved nirvana before my eyes.

I wonder if all therapists are as mercurial as Shara-Rose, who insists that she's completely in control of her shifting moods and that, during sessions, she consciously tries out different approaches with her patients. But I'm not convinced. I think she's moody and volatile, just like me.

"I'm feeling ambivalent," I tell her.

"I see. You're feeling ambivalent," she repeats calmly.

"Right. I'm feeling ambivalent about everything. Not just the journal. About George. Even though I _know_ I'm doing the right thing by not speaking to him, I feel sort of ambivalent anyway. And I'm also ambivalent about babies. And about you. Maya. Jay. TAG. My own current state of sexual fidelity, including my not going off with Trent Johnson yesterday in that tight T-shirt.... About everything."

Her mood seems to shift again: Now she's leaning forward aggressively, blowing smoke at me, transforming herself into one of those obnoxiously bossy shrinks, the kind who want to run their patients' lives. "Well, I'm telling you right out," she says flatly, "that one thing about which you'd better not be ambivalent is couple counseling."

I'm brought up short. "What?"

"You heard me. You and George need to try to work things out. And couple counseling could help."

"How could you possibly counsel George," I ask indignantly, "when you and he used to be in a therapy group together?"

"Not me," she says, lighting a second crushed cigarette, ignoring the tobacco flakes descending on her catsuit, "someone who's never laid eyes on either of you before."

I see an exaggerated, cartoonlike picture in my mind: George and I are sitting side by side on an ugly tweed sofa, our hands rigidly folded on our laps. The shrink is sitting across from us in a big armchair with enormous armrests. With a great flourish, he strokes his bushy white beard. "Your trouble," he says loudly to me, in a fake German accent, "is that you weren't breast-fed when you were an infant. As a result, you are too needy. You expect too much from George. You think he is a...what was the name of that singing group again...a Beatle!" "You-you-you said it, Doc," the cartoon George smugly interjects, sounding just like Bugs Bunny.

"No," I say firmly to Shara-Rose. "There's no way I'm going for couple counseling with George. Individual therapy, journal therapy, couple therapy! It's just too much. Besides, honestly, I have *nothing* to say to George, nothing to discuss. He did what he did, and I responded the way I did: action–reaction. All I want to do is go back to Lydia's and be alone and watch TV."

"Our time is up," Shara-Rose announces cheerily, rising and walking me to the door. "And don't eat the pint of chocolate chocolate chip, okay?" Her expression is mischievous. "Your clothes aren't going to fit if you keep this up."

14

When I return to Lydia's apartment, Flaca seems agitated, but I can't figure out why. I stand in Lydia's doorway and look around. Things appear to be just as they were when I left for my appointment with Shara-Rose this morning: the directors' chairs, the dolls, the framed photo on the wall of Lydia eating cotton candy in Disneyland when she was about ten, long before she could have possibly dreamed that she was going to grow up to become a celebrated performance artist.

But Flaca is no hysteric, and if she's upset, there's got to be a good reason for it. She begins to circle around me, a feline Lassie. "Show me what's wrong, Flaca," I say. In obedient Lassie fashion, she waddles toward the large bedroom. I follow her.

I stand in the bedroom doorway, and I can't believe my eyes: The room is crammed full with things that weren't there before. A bulging canvas suitcase in the middle of the floor. A guitar leaning upright against the full-length mirror on the wall. A pair of black sneakers sitting on the bed. A dungaree jacket draped over the back of an orange director's chair. I know that Lydia is doing an interview on the West Coast today, so I'm sure she hasn't returned.

I try to gather my courage to go inside the room. I pick Flaca up and hold her against my chest, and together, our hearts beating in rhythm, we enter.

Immediately, she struggles free of my arms and climbs up into an orange director's chair. She yawns, and almost instantly falls asleep, a very un-Lassie-like thing to do.

I walk over to the bed and stare at the black sneakers. They're long and narrow, meant for the bony feet of some tall, wiry male. Definitely not Lydia. The guitar, the dungaree jacket, the sneakers: I picture a terrifying-looking singer from a heavy-metal band—not my type of rock star at all.

I drag the suitcase over to the bed and begin rummaging inside. The first thing I come upon is a pair of men's black bikini underpants. Then a pair of aviator-shaped mirrored sunglasses. I rummage some more and I pull out a cheap-looking paperback, *The Hot Tomato Murders*, with a cover illustration of a redheaded woman wearing a low-cut dress the color of ripe tomatoes. Maybe the intruder is a homicidal heavy-metal rock star.

I sit down on the edge of the bed and look at Flaca, who's still asleep. I wish that, like her, I could just fall into a deep sleep, and that when I awoke, poof, all of this would be gone. But most of all, I wish that my life were simple and secure again, the way it was before George strayed.

Warily, I get up and remove the dungaree jacket from the back of the chair, trying not to disturb Flaca, who stirs but doesn't wake up. I try it on. I look at myself in the mirror over Lydia's cluttered bureau, hoping for a clue to the owner's identity. The sleeves are a little long, but other than that the jacket fits pretty well. And then I hear the front door opening. First the top lock. Then the bottom.

My heart is pounding. I should have had the sense to run away, rather than to have hung around trying on the intruder's clothes.

But it's too late for that. I swoop Flaca up from the chair, fiercely determined to protect her at all costs. I hold her tightly. She looks at me with sleepy surprise.

I look around the room for a weapon. The only thing I see is a pair of knife-sharp ruby-red shoes sitting in an open shoebox on top of Lydia's bureau next to a blue-eyed baby doll in diapers. I remember these shoes. Lydia wore them for one of her pieces, a contemporary retelling of _Cinderella_. Even Nicole Burden's Fuck-Me shoes are wimps compared to these. These shoes could easily poke a man's eyes out or stab him through the heart. And I'm ready to do both of these things if I have to. I won't go down without a fight. Imagining that the intruder is George, toward whom I've been harboring violent urges anyway, I grab one of the shoes. I grip it tightly with one hand, still clinging to Flaca with the other, and I hide behind the door.

Flaka is awake now, squirming in my arms. I hear footsteps. I'm one inch away from screaming at the top of my lungs, or fainting dead away. How did my life suddenly become a page right out of _The Hot Tomato Murders?_

The footsteps are nearer. He's coming inside, and this is it. No time for hesitation. With a strangled, panicked cry, I leap forward from behind the door, determined to maim and kill with Lydia's Mega-Fuck-Me shoe.

But the man barging into the room makes an equally strangled, panicked cry. He kicks the shoe right out of my hand. The shoe flies across the room and lands on top of the bed.

Flaca looks terrified. She jumps from my arms and races out the bedroom door, moving faster than she has in years.

"Babette," Carlos Carlos stands in the doorway, panting and staring at me as though I'm insane, "what's going on?"

My heart begins to slow down. "Carlos," I ask, after a minute, once I can find my voice, "why are you here?" I don't sound much like a welcoming committee, but I don't care.

"Sorry about the kick," Carlos says, looking a little sheepish. "I've been studying Kung Fu." He pauses. "Didn't Lydia tell you?"

"Tell me what?"

"Oh." He looks uncomfortable. "She told me that she was going to tell you." He looks around. "I would have taken the smaller bedroom but your stuff was already there. I wish she'd told you."

"Told me what?" I say flatly, although I'm beginning to have a hunch that I know, and I don't like it one bit.

He confirms my hunch. "I'm going to be staying here, too. We're going to be roommates."

15

Carlos goes into the bathroom to wash up.

Still wearing his dungaree jacket, I sit down heavily on the bed. The very last thing in the world I want is a roommate. And even if I did want a roommate, the adulterous Carlos Carlos wouldn't be my top choice. Although, from what I've heard, Carlos and Jay's ex-wife, Martha, have been living happily together since Martha left Jay for Carlos. Even Jay seems to forgive them. Or maybe he just pretends to. But—even if I'm beginning to be a bit self-righteous, like all reformed sinners—I resent Carlos, especially right now. I can't help but equate him with Nicole Burden.

Besides, there's something else about him that's always made me uncomfortable: his name. Carlos Carlos is not Latino in any way, shape, or form. He's from Connecticut, he went to Harvard, even if he never did graduate, and somewhere along the line he borrowed—or stole?—this name from another culture. I've always suspected that he uses the name to get grants from organizations that award money to minority artists. Or to make himself seem exotic to women.

I walk into the kitchen, where the Barbie Doll on the table is still poised to deliver her backhand. I press the Play button on Lydia's answering machine. Lydia's own voice comes on loud and clear, as though she's here in the room with me. She must have left this message while I was at my session with Shara-Rose. "Babette," she says, sounding, as always, absolutely confident of herself, "I know that you won't mind that Carlos Carlos is going to be staying at my place too. He's so hard-working, you won't even notice him. God, this touring stuff is exhausting. I may give up performing and go back to school and get an MBA."

I don't believe for one moment that Lydia will go back to school and get an MBA. I also don't believe for one moment that I won't notice Carlos Carlos. He's already made an unforgettable entrance.

A second message comes on. Predictably, it's George's message of the day. "Babette," he says, "I have an idea. Maybe we should see someone together. A counselor. To help us sort things through. We've got to talk. We can't just end things without talking."

I'm enraged. Either he's spoken to Shara-Rose, or else he too believes that therapy—Ye Olde Talking Cure—is a panacea, that all people need to do is express their feelings, and—voilà—life is beautiful. Well, they're wrong: Therapy is no panacea, and it can't magically erase the past.

But his message isn't over. He begins to sing. This time the song is "She Loves You," although he's changed it to "He Loves You." I wonder if he's planning on systematically destroying the Beatles' entire oeuvre for me.

I feel a hand on my shoulder.

"I guess he loves you," Carlos says.

I feel even angrier. It's bad enough that George had an affair with Nicole Burden and then was too cowardly and deceitful to tell me, and that I've left him, and that soon I'm going to have to do one of the most horrible things there is to do in New York City—

apartment hunt—and that George is on this weird kick of singing Beatles' songs over the answering machine in order to woo me back, but the idea that Carlos Carlos, my new roommate, is going to be using the answering machine and will be hearing George's songs too is just too much for me to bear. I burst into tears.

"Hey," Carlos says, and he puts his arms around me.

Despite the fact that I don't trust him, I allow him to hold me. Weeping all over his chest, I feel grateful to him, against my better instincts. Finally I stop crying. Trying to muster some dignity, I remove myself from Carlos's arms and I sit down at the kitchen table.

Carlos sits across from me. He leans his elbows on the table. "Babette," he says, "in all the times I've seen you working at TAG, I've never seen you lose your poise and self-control, not even for a second, not even when you were working yourself to the brink of exhaustion. Which I've seen you do many times there. Martha always said she envied you for being so together."

I can't believe my ears: Martha, the beautiful earth mother with the serene, unwrinkled forehead? Martha, who can bake a sourdough loaf with one hand and whip up a frothy soufflé with the other, envying me?

"Something must really be wrong, for you to be so overwrought."

I might as well tell him. After all, as the injured party in the Babette-George-Nicole triangle, I've got nothing to hide. "I've left George," I say. "That's why I'm staying here."

Carlos doesn't say anything.

"George was having an affair." I wonder how he'll take this, whether it will elicit a guilty response. But he simply scratches his slim, patrician nose. Carlos looks more like a Classics professor at a small, respectable New England college than a member of the New York avant-garde. All the black bikini underwear, mirrored sunglasses, and dungaree jackets in the world can't change that fact. I tell him about my lunch with Nicole, and my drunken confrontation with George, and my running off with Flaca, and how

I'm not willing to speak to George, even if my shrink, my sister, and George himself, all seem to think "I'm a little bit crazy."

Carlos doesn't say a word. So I tell him about my ambivalence about having a child, and about Jay's anger at me because I'm not working at TAG this summer, and about my frustration because I'd like to do something truly significant with my life but I can't figure out what, and about my own hard-earned monogamy in marriage. I even tell him, without naming names, that just the other day one of the actors in his play, *Early Man*, came on to me at my health club, and how difficult it was for me to resist—and yet, how I did, finally, resist. And then I tell him about how I don't want to start couple therapy, because I believe that the silence in my marriage is now an impenetrable one.

I'm absolutely exhausted from describing my problems, my sorrows, my temptations, and my rage. "Carlos," I ask bluntly, "what about you? Why are you here?" I lean back, making it clear that it's his turn.

"Martha," he begins, without a second's hesitation, "threw me out. The other night, out of the blue, she told me that for the last three months she's been having an affair with the guy she dated all through high school. Her 'high school honey,' she calls him." He pauses. "He's a *lawyer*."

I take another deep breath. Carlos's story is starting to sound awfully close to home.

"Martha asked me," Carlos says sadly, "to move out of the loft, which is in her name, as soon as possible. She wanted her high school honey to move right in."

Before I can feel one hundred percent sympathetic, before I can possibly even go so far as to empathize with him, there's one thing I have to know. "Carlos, why did you change your name?"

He doesn't appear to be surprised, almost as though he knows why I'm asking. "My father was a minister," he answers matter-of-factly, and he picks the Barbie Doll up from the table and begins rocking her in his arms, "and he expected me to become a minister, too. But I was reading Jack Kerouac, chasing after girls, listening to Lou Reed, and the last thing I wanted was to become a man of the cloth. I realized that I'd never be able to live without guilt unless I disassociated myself from my past. So when I was eighteen I changed my name to one that was so far removed from my parents and their world that it freed me. By becoming Carlos Carlos, I became alive." He looks embarrassed, as though he's just become aware that he's a grown man holding onto a doll for comfort. He places Barbie back on the tabletop.

I go to the refrigerator and remove the pint of chocolate chocolate chip from the freezer. I hack away at it with a spoon until I succeed in dividing it equally into two bowls. We sit at the kitchen table and eat the ice cream. Neither of us speaks. When he's finished with his ice cream, he licks his lips and finally breaks the silence. "I'm working on a piece," he says, "that I was hoping would debut at TAG in the fall, but now, with Acme Developers hovering around, and arts funding being cut right and left, who knows?"

I lick my spoon. It's enough for me to empathize with his romantic problems. I don't want to start empathizing with his artistic ones.

"It's called *Hard-Boiled*," he says, "and it's sort of a loving parody of those really trashy paperback detective novels. I used to read them voraciously when I was a kid. I still do, sometimes."

I lick the spoon some more. At least that explains *The Hot Tomato Murders*.

"Work is really the best therapy in the world for me. When I'm working, I tend to become so completely absorbed that I stop dwelling on my problems. That's what I'm hoping will happen this time, too. What are *you* working on?" he asks.

"My journal," I say brightly. I tell him all about Shara-Rose's journal therapy idea, sounding far more enthused about it than I really am. I don't mention my writing anxiety. "That's interesting."

He looks almost shy. "Would you mind if I borrowed the idea? Maybe I can work it into *Hard-Boiled*."

"Feel free," I say, "although it's really my therapist's idea, not mine." I can't imagine how Carlos will be able to work journal therapy into a play about hard-boiled detectives, but that's his business, not mine.

He stands. "Well, thanks for everything—the idea, the ice cream, and the talk. I'm going to work."

He washes his own bowl in the sink, which bodes well for a harmonious roommate situation. He heads toward Lydia's bedroom. I hear him close the bedroom door, but after that I don't hear a thing. I feel envious. I imagine him sitting on Lydia's bed, hunched over a notebook, absorbed in the creation of *Hard-Boiled*.

16

Carlos and I have been roommates for ten days. I'm still not completely reconciled to his being here, although Shara-Rose thinks that it's good for me to have company. Not that Carlos Carlos is all that much company; he's much too busy working on *Hard-Boiled*, which he's determined to finish by the end of the summer, before the small amount of grant money he received from Astro Arts—a foundation dedicated to helping innovative theater artists—runs out and he has to go back to driving a taxi.

Despite my initial distrust of him, he's behaving very decently. Yesterday, for instance, he fed Flaca in the morning, before I woke up. And he's offered never to listen to any of the messages on Lydia's answering machine before I've had a chance to listen to them first. That way, I can erase George's daily messages before he hears them. George is no longer singing Beatles songs. Now his messages are sometimes pleading, sometimes angry, and sometimes seductive. When he sounds seductive, it's hardest for me to resist him, although I'm determined not to be swayed by something as superficial as the sound of a voice. After all, even the voice-overs on TV commercials for dog food can sound seductive.

Tonight, however, Carlos and I are deviating from our routine. Tonight we're going to an East Village club called Tarts to hear Mild Neurosis, Shara-Rose's group, play. I heard an ad for their performance on the radio, and I taped a note on Carlos's door, asking him to come with me. I didn't mention that I didn't have the courage to go alone, because Shara-Rose had specifically asked me, when I first began therapy, not to go to any of her performances. "I keep my musician life separate from my patients, Babette," she'd said. "I'm a traditional enough shrink, in my own way. Agreed?" I'd agreed. But right now, in my time of crisis, I've decided to go back on my word.

Carlos is waiting for me by the front door. "Martha and I liked to go to clubs a lot," he says, "but I've never heard of Tarts." He adjusts his mirrored sunglasses.

I smooth my sleeveless black linen dress over my hips, fluff my vampy Veronica Lake hairdo with my fingers, and kneel down and plant a good-bye kiss on the top of Flaca's head. I follow Carlos out into the street, now worrying that Shara-Rose will be furious when she sees me in the audience. But I'm just following her advice. "Stop indulging in your misery," she keeps saying, "go out and start doing things!"

Carlos steps into the street to hail a cab, while I hand out quarters. As usual, there are too many people for me to give quarters to all of them. So tonight I choose to give to those who appear the most agitated and disturbed, the ones talking and gesticulating to themselves.

We get into a cab. The driver's hair is swept into a dramatic pompadour. He looks at us in his rearview mirror as he speeds down Ninth Avenue. "Man, this is turning into a nice neighborhood," he says. "You folks own or rent?"

Carlos and I look embarrassedly at each other, aware that he thinks we're a couple.

"We're apartment sitting for someone who's away," Carlos says.

The driver loses interest, and he concentrates instead on veering wildly in and out of lanes and running red lights.

Finally, we're way downtown and very far east, and the cab screeches to a halt outside Tarts. Although Carlos and I split the fare, he offers to pay the tip, which is another decent thing for him to do, since I know that the money he's living on from Astro Arts is pretty meager.

Tarts turns out to be a street-level club with no doorman and no line outside, although the club across the street, Zenith, has a burly doorman in a white silk jacket and a line of people snaking around the otherwise desolate block.

Tarts consists of a bar and a back room. The bar is empty. The bartender, whose hair is dyed a flat yellow, is wearing an iron cross around his neck. He's staring up at a blank TV screen above the bar. He doesn't notice us as we walk past.

In the back room, there are about two dozen small tables, and no stage that I can see, although some drums are set up at one end of the room. The walls are decorated with black-and-white photographs of women with teased hair, false eyelashes, and slinky dresses: "tarts" from Grade B fifties movies.

A blond boy who looks underage is sitting at a table in the center of the room. He's wearing a ripped sweatshirt that says, "He Lives!" beneath a portrait of a pouty-lipped Jim Morrison. The boy is staring gloomily down at the tabletop. I have a suspicion that he, like me, is a patient of Shara-Rose's who couldn't resist coming to hear her sing.

At the only other occupied table, two men are sipping frozen blue margaritas. One of them, who has short red hair, is wearing a seersucker suit, and the other, who has short brown hair, is wearing a light gray jacket. They look tense. I decide that they're lovers who are in couple therapy with Shara-Rose.

The rest of the tables are empty.

I lead the way to a dark corner table. If we're way back, I think, maybe Shara-Rose won't spot me.

A waiter approaches. He's neat and preppy in a sparkling white polo shirt and pressed khaki slacks. He's probably a college student who's also in therapy with Shara-Rose.

"Anything to drink?" the waiter asks, and I wonder why I'm so determined to convince myself that he, and everyone else in the room, is a patient of Shara-Rose's. I guess I'm trying to share my guilt about coming here in spite of my agreement not to.

"Whiskey, straight," Carlos mumbles to the waiter. He looks even more depressed than usual. He's probably remembering all the happy moments that he and Martha shared in clubs like this. I order a seltzer, trying to put aside any more thoughts about the waiter and Shara-Rose. Instead, I wonder how to cheer Carlos up. More and more, I'm starting to like him. But I'm so down in the dumps myself, it's probably impossible for me to cheer anyone else up. Still, I want to try. "At least you and Martha weren't legally married." As soon as the words are out of my mouth, I wish I hadn't said them. They're not really terribly cheery. Or nice.

He looks up at me. "At least you have some of your pride left. You left George. I was dumped."

I grope for something to say that will help avoid an argument about which of us has it worse. "Well, at least neither of us has children who'll be devastated by the breakup of their parents."

"Right," he says grimly, "but the night Martha asked me to leave, she also mentioned that she and her high-school honey want to have a child by next year."

Now we're both feeling much worse.

A few more people wander in. The place is so tiny it's starting to feel full.

The preppy waiter brings us our drinks.

I'm still determined to try to cheer Carlos up. It's possible that if _he_ feels better, I'll feel better. I lift my glass of seltzer. "Carlos, I'd like to propose a toast."

Still looking morbidly depressed, he lifts his whiskey glass. "To your success with _Hard-Boiled._" We gently clink our glasses.

For the first time since he's moved into Lydia's, he smiles. He removes his mirrored sunglasses and slips them into the pocket of his dungaree jacket. "And here's a toast to you, Babette," he says. "To your bliss."

We clink our glasses again.

Also for the first time, I notice how very attractive Carlos is, how his dungaree jacket fits him snugly and sexily, and how his patrician nose is so straight and elegant. And I sense that he's suddenly noticing that I'm not half bad either. I run a hand through my hair, trying to fluff it up a bit more. Yes, I suddenly think, Carlos is the one I should have my first extramarital fling with! We're already living together, and he never leaves his dishes in the sink expecting me to wash them. It definitely makes more sense than my having gone off with Trent, a.k.a. Org, or any of the other actors from _Early Man._ It also makes more sense than my poring through my old address books and tracking down some of those sculptors, ad writers, chiropractors, and unemployed actors from my past—something else I've been contemplating doing lately. I've even entertained thoughts of trying to track down Ricky, the weasel from high school, and having an affair with him—whatever his current "look" is—and then dumping him first this time, getting revenge on him for both Maya and myself.

But no, I'm sure that Carlos is the one to seriously consider. I start to fantasize about what he's like in bed—tender but aggressive, I decide, sensitive but wild. After all, the person who created _Early Man_ must have a pretty virile streak in him. And just then, as I'm imagining myself wrapping my legs around Carlos's slim waist, I spot George, sitting at a table across the room and watching me.

17

In what seems like less than an instant, George crosses the room and is standing over me, and I feel as though I'm having a heart attack. I've got all the symptoms. Shooting pains, left arm. Agonizing pain, chest. Breathing, difficult. Speech, impossible. Death, imminent?

"Hello, Babette," George says, "I'm surprised to see you here." His soft, measured voice is trembling slightly.

Fortunately, my heart attack symptoms begin to subside. My left arm and my chest feel almost normal, and I take a deep breath. Whether I like it or not, I'm going to live to endure this meeting with George, my husband and betrayer, whose trembling voice has touched me, despite my resolve never again to allow him to touch me, physically or emotionally, and whose timing for showing up in my life couldn't be much worse. I move my chair closer to Carlos.

Also, despite my resolve never again to find George handsome, I do. He's wearing a striped blazer, his blue jeans look newly washed, and he has a fetching trace of five-o'clock shadow. He reminds me of the way Beatle George looks nowadays on his comeback rock videos—which I've been watching at Lydia's—with his own fetching chin stubble.

Carlos and George seem to be sizing each other up. I'm not sure whether they recognize each other. At most, they've probably met a few times at TAG.

George takes an empty chair from a nearby table and pulls it up to our table. He sits down. I move my chair even closer to Carlos. Life is very weird indeed, when George, my husband, is my enemy, and Carlos, whom I barely know, is my closest ally.

"You're George," Carlos says at last. He looks uncomfortable. He's probably afraid that I'm going to try to kill George on the spot. After all, not too long ago he himself was attacked with Lydia's shoe, and that was just for leaving his suitcase in Lydia's room.

George is staring at Carlos. His expression is odd. As a lawyer, George has pretty well learned to master the art of looking inscrutable when he needs to, but his face looks violent with emotion now, although I can't quite figure out what emotion.

I find my voice. "George, this is Carlos Carlos. You remember, he wrote and directed _Early Man?_" I sound exaggeratedly polite.

"I remember." George doesn't sound nearly as polite. His voice isn't trembling any longer. He sounds just like the kind of lawyer he's prided himself on not becoming—loud, brassy, and arrogant.

And that's when I figure out what the emotion is that's distorting his features. It's jealousy, of course. Like the cab driver, he thinks that Carlos and I are a couple. The other day, in my fantasy about George discovering me with Trent Johnson, I was happy that he was jealous, but in real life it infuriates me. What nerve he has, thinking that in less than two weeks I'm already having an affair, even if, in fact, I was just fantasizing about that very thing myself. Because the truth is, I haven't had one, and if he actually thinks I've already begun sleeping around, then he's not acknowledging my very real suffering, my loneliness, and my grieving.

Which I'm definitely entitled to, despite my own indiscretions during my single days, and despite the fact that some people are finding my reponse to his one so-called fling "a little bit crazy." *Well, crazy is as crazy does,* I mumble aloud, senselessly—still in a rage—but nobody seems to hear me, because just then the waiter returns, asking us all if we'd like another round.

Carlos orders a second whiskey. George orders a beer. I look at Carlos. I look at George. I look at the waiter. This is going to be a long night. "A vodka, straight," I order.

George looks concerned. After all, he must recall my drunken state the day of his confession about Nicole Burden. He looks at Carlos with irritation, as though it's Carlos who's dragging me down into the gutter of alcoholism. This only enrages me more. George, the betrayer, blaming innocent, shell-shocked Carlos. Besides, George should only know the truth, which is that alcohol isn't really my weakness at all. It's ice cream.

Carlos is looking at George with an equally irritated expression, as though he knows what George is accusing him of and doesn't like it one bit.

"Babette," George says, leaning toward me, ignoring Carlos completely, "I want to talk to you. I *intend* to talk to you."

The waiter returns and sets our drinks down on the table. I take three quick sips of the vodka. And now, instead of heart attack pain, I feel intense heat in my chest. "Carlos and I just couldn't resist coming to see Shara-Rose tonight, could we, Carlos?" My voice is coy and flirtatious—with a Scarlett O'Hara lilt—reminding me more of Maya's voice than of my own. Carlos raises his eyebrows. George also raises his eyebrows. I take a fourth sip of the vodka. And a fifth. And that's when I do it: the unthinkable, the unfathomable. Something that only the devil could make me do. I reach over and I lay my hand caressingly on Carlos's hand, right in front of George.

I leave my hand there. I even squeeze Carlos's hand slightly.

I'm sure Carlos understands that I'm doing this only because I'm now determined to make George even more jealous than he already is. Painfully jealous. I want him to be the one to have the real heart attack at our table.

Carlos, looking uneasy, disengages his hand from mine. He stands and excuses himself. I stare across the table at George, who's looking increasingly intense, the way Beatle George must have looked back when Eric Clapton stole Patti Boyd from him, although, I have to remind myself, Eric Clapton didn't exactly "shoplift" Patti Boyd off the dress rack at Alexander's—she went with him "voluntarily," of her own free will.

George leans toward me. And, as though he's a magnet and I'm a piece of metal, I immediately want to lean forward right into his arms. But I also want to defy the law of magnetic attraction and lean backwards, far away from him. What I do instead is freeze, and I remember one of Maya's old diary entries: "Dear Diary, my little sister Babette is so namby-pamby, she never knows what she wants!!!"

Carlos returns to the table. I don't take his hand this time.

Meanwhile, George is shaking his head, looking confused and angry and pained all at once. He seems about to speak to me, but just then, with no warm-up and no introduction, Mild Neurosis comes riding into the room on a tidal wave of sound, making the loudest music I've ever heard in my life.

George and I are both rendered speechless. We stare at Mild Neurosis, which consists of a drummer, two guitarists, and Shara-Rose.

The drummer looks like a Hell's Angel. He's chunky and bearded, wearing a T-shirt with a skull and crossbones on the front. He places a six-pack of beer on top of his drums. One of the guitarists is balding. He's wearing tortoiseshell eyeglasses. He looks like a mild-mannered accountant who wandered into Tarts by mistake.

The second guitarist is a teenage girl. She looks like a punk ballerina, with her short spiky hair, shining Lycra tights, and a black skirt shaped like a tutu.

But it's Shara-Rose, of course, standing in front of the others and belting out a song, that I can't take my eyes off. She's pinned a bunch of small white flowers in her curly red hair, and she's wearing big black earrings that look like bowling balls. Her dress is red leather, short, with a metallic zipper that stretches from top to bottom. I feel myself smiling. I feel proud of her. My shrink. Onstage. In bright red leather. Singing her heart out.

She's shouting into the mike, moving her whole body to the music. I strain to make out the words of her song over the pounding beat of the drums and the guitars. But I can only make out bits and pieces, something like, "You seem okay baby / though you may be in pain / so don't look my way baby / 'cause you may be insane...."

The music is so overwhelming that it's impossible for me to worry about George. Mild Neurosis does about four or five more songs. The songs all seem to blend into one another, all of a piece, like a live concept album. They're all about the pain of love and craziness, two subjects I think about a lot these days.

The music is so intense that I feel as though Shara-Rose and Mild Neurosis have cast a spell on me. And I love it. George can't touch me now. Nobody can. I'm untouchable. I lean my head back, eager to let Shara-Rose and Mild Neurosis work their magic on me.

Carlos, however, immediately breaks the spell. Because this time it's he who does the unfathomable: It's he who reaches over and takes my hand. Which means that I *can* be touched, after all. I'm still vulnerable. I wait for lightning—or for George—to strike me down. But instead, George merely stares at our linked hands in horror, as though cockroaches are crawling on them.

"We'll take a brief break," I hear Shara-Rose saying into the mike. I look up at her. She's looking right back at me, and she isn't smiling.

18

There's nothing magical or spellbinding about Shara-Rose as she strides quickly toward our table, puffing on a cigarette. She hasn't cracked a friendly smile in my direction yet. She pulls up a chair next to George. The table feels even more crowded than before.

I keep waiting for George to explode. But so far, nothing. My hand, in Carlos's hand, is sweaty.

Squinting, Shara-Rose wipes her forehead. She takes a drag of her cigarette. She stares at my hand, although she doesn't say anything.

I feel embarrassed, and I remove my hand from Carlos's hand. Carlos doesn't look uneasy now. In fact, he's smiling. He seems to be enjoying himself.

"By the way, Babette," Shara-Rose says, "what brings you here in the first place?" Her voice is calm.

I try to meet her gaze, but I can't. I drop my eyes. I take a small sip of vodka. "I heard an ad on the radio."

"So, okay," she replies, "you heard an ad. But that doesn't

explain why you came." Her voice is still calm, but I'm sure she's angry at me for breaking our agreement.

I look around the club. I point to the boy in the Jim Morrison sweatshirt, who's holding his chin in his hand and scowling. "Well, he's also a patient of yours, isn't he?"

She blows some smoke at me. "Never saw the kid before in my life."

"Well, what about them?" I point to the tense-looking men, still sipping their blue margaritas.

Shara-Rose looks impatient. "Never saw them before, either."

The preppy waiter comes over. He's my last hope. "What about him?" I ask.

"Hi," he says to Shara-Rose, "I'm on my break."

"Hi," she smiles, "pull up a chair. George," she says, "this is Ronnie." She doesn't introduce Ronnie to me and Carlos.

George appears recovered from the experience of having seen me and Carlos holding hands. He looks mellow, as though he's never experienced a moment's painful jealousy in his life. He's probably decided that my little hand-holding escapade was a bit of harmless mischief, nothing more. Or maybe he just doesn't want to let me see any more of his pain. Or maybe being silent about his feelings is just too strong a habit to break. He politely shakes Ronnie's hand.

"Listen, Ronnie," I say impatiently, "you're a patient of Shara-Rose's, aren't you?"

Ronnie looks surprised.

Shara-Rose squints and blows some more smoke in my direction. "Ronnie isn't my patient," she says icily. "He's my lover."

I feel as though I'm experiencing an existential dilemma: Like, why in the world am I here, sitting in this firetrap club with my estranged husband, my strange new roommate, my even stranger shrink, and her college-age lover? But before I can resolve my existential dilemma, the other members of Mild Neurosis—the beer-

guzzling drummer, the balding guitarist, and the teenage punk-bal-
lerina guitarist—descend upon us. Without being invited, they pull
up an empty table and adjoin it to ours. "I'm Rambo," the drummer
announces, in a surprisingly high-pitched voice. He scratches his
armpit and takes a swig of beer. "And this is Mike and Gracey."

"George," George says politely, offering his hand to Rambo.

I feel something warm on my knee. A hand. It has to be
Carlos's hand, since George, across the table, has one hand in
Rambo's paw, and the other around his beer glass.

There's no way that this surreptitious gesture of Carlos's can be
interpreted as a friendly attempt to help me make George jealous.
It's a private gesture, intended just for me. So it must be a sexual
come-on. Unless I'm misreading him completely, and it's only his
innocent way of saying, "Hang on, Babette, I'm your new pal, and
I'm here for you."

George is leaning across the table and saying something to me.
He seems unaware of Carlos's hand on my knee. And I'm grateful
for that. Because even a polite lawyer from Sioux City might be
driven to commit murder if he knew that his wife was allowing a
man she barely knows to caress her knee right under his nose.
Even a polite, adulterous lawyer. "Babette, Shara-Rose invited me
to come hear her sing tonight," George says seriously, "because she
wanted me to get out and stop dwelling on my unhappiness." This
sounds suspiciously similar to the advice she gave me. Except, of
course, she didn't invite me to come hear her sing tonight. Before
I can reply to George, Ronnie turns to me. "I hear," he says, "that
you work at TAG. Well, I'm an actor." He smiles.

He seems to expect me to say something. "Congratulations." I
try to sound sincere.

"When I work, and, obviously," he looks ruefully around the
club, "I'm not working now, but when I do I usually play teenage
boys because I look so much younger than I am. Would you believe
I'm almost thirty-one?"

"No," I answer honestly, "I took you for a college student." It's difficult to accept that this boyish young waiter is really an out-of-work actor. It's also difficult to accept that Carlos's hand is still on my knee, and that it's moving slightly higher.

"I'd *love* to be working now," Ronnie says to me, with so much urgency that I wonder if he's about to hand me his résumé and some head shots.

Carlos's hand is now on my lower thigh. I steal a glance at him. His expression is impassive.

I turn back to Ronnie. "Would I have seen you in anything?" I ask, trying to sound casual, and trying not to focus on the sensation of Carlos's hand beneath my dress, resting on my goosebump-covered skin.

"Well," Ronnie says, smiling from ear to ear, "I did a blue jeans commercial a year ago that got a lot of play."

Carlos's hand moves up to my midthigh.

"Sorry," I say to Ronnie, breathing rapidly and trying not to let my glance wander across the table to George, "I don't remember that one."

Gracey, who until now has seemed totally oblivious, becomes animated. "I remember! You were the guy who climbs the mountain to show that the jeans won't split, right?"

The balding guitarist, Mike, who also hasn't said a word until now, looks annoyed. "No," he says crossly, "that was a much younger guy, a *real* kid."

Rambo looks at me. "Hey," he says, helping himself to a cigarette from Shara-Rose's pack, "are you a friend of Shara-Rose's?" He slides the pack across the table to me, as though I appear desperately in need of a cigarette.

"No," I reply, ignoring the cigarettes, "I'm her…"

Before I can finish, Carlos moves his hand even higher. Much higher. I feel nervous and guilty. And more than slightly exhilarated.

Carlos leans over and whispers in my ear, "Let's get out of here."

His breath is warm. I shiver slightly.

George looks at me. "Feeling cold?" he asks, politely. "Would you like to borrow my jacket?"

I shake my head. I can't tell whether George is being genuinely solicitous or whether he knows exactly what's going on.

Shara-Rose is reaching across the table for her cigarette pack, but Gracey, crossing her legs, knocks one of her bony knees into the tabletop, causing the pack to fall beneath the table. "Shit," Shara-Rose says. She bends down to retrieve it. Carlos's hand is now moving in a gentle circular motion on the very top of my thigh, faster and faster.

When Shara-Rose emerges from beneath the table, she has an unlit cigarette between her lips. She looks at me with one of her impassive expressions, although she must have seen Carlos's hand.

I rise abruptly, upsetting my glass of vodka. Luckily, it's empty. "Carlos and I were just leaving," I announce. I feel myself blushing.

George's expression is unreadable. "Have a nice evening," he says evenly. "I'll call you, Babette."

"It was nice meeting all of you," Carlos says, sounding very professorial and dignified. He slips on his undignified mirrored sunglasses and begins to steer me out of the room.

At the door, we practically collide into Jay and Maya. Maya appears slightly dazed: Going to downtown clubs isn't exactly her thing.

"Oh," Jay says, "the two roomies."

I wait for him to say something to Carlos about Martha's dumping him, maybe to commiserate about her fickleness, or to stick out his tongue and say, "Nyah, nyah, serves you right." Instead, he says to me, "Sarah and I could _really_ use your help organizing the demonstration, Babette." He pauses, then adds sarcastically, "Maybe I haven't mentioned this to you before."

I ignore his sarcasm. "What are you two doing here?"

"I heard an ad on the radio," he admits, now sounding slightly sheepish and not at all sarcastic. "And I thought that Maya would enjoy hearing Shara-Rose sing."

"Well, go on in," I urge. "I'm sure Shara-Rose will be absolutely *delighted* to see you both."

Carlos takes my arm, and we step outside. The not-so-fresh air feels genuinely refreshing.

19

Carlos steps out into the middle of the street to hail a cab. I linger in the doorway of Tarts, taking deep breaths to clear my head. Suddenly Maya appears at my side, scowling. "Babette, I came out here to have a private talk with you." She doesn't wait for my response. "Look, I really don't blame you for wanting a little something on the side right now, but not with *that* guy." She points at Carlos, who's standing in the middle of the street, waving both arms and unsuccessfully trying to flag down what appears to be an entire fleet of off-duty cabs.

"Why *not* with him?" I'm curious. Not because I care about Maya's taste in men, and certainly not because I would ever heed her romantic advice, but because her perceptions about the world always fascinate me, one way or another.

"Well, it's obvious. He's a callous womanizer. First he put the moves on Martha, when she was still with Jay. Now he's moving in on you while you're *still* married, even if you insist upon going through with this crazy idea of not speaking to your own husband.

And then he'll leave you and move right in on someone else before you can blink an eye. My guess is that he'll come after *me* next, to get back at Jay again."

I don't have a clue why Maya thinks Carlos wants to "get back" at Jay, but the very thought of Carlos and Maya together renders me speechless.

"And also," Maya continues, "this ridiculous name he's given himself—*Carlos Carlos*—as though he's a real Spanish dreamboat, like Ricardo Montalban…"

I'm growing angry. Carlos is many things, but he's no callous womanizer. That's clear to me from the nights he's been locked in his room working on *Hard-Boiled*, and also how hurt he is by Martha, whom he clearly loved. And although I don't want to try to explain it to Maya, I've come to understand why Carlos needed to change his name in order to change his life. "Don't worry, Maya." My voice is tense. "Carlos is my new roommate. That's all."

She shrugs. "Yeah, right, and like, I was born yesterday." Suddenly she sounds a lot less like her usual breathless faux Scarlett O'Hara, and a lot more like the shoplifting kid from the Bronx she once was. I find this endearing, and I feel less angry. "Lighten up, Maya." I air-kiss her cheek, so that her rouge doesn't get on me. I walk out into the street to join Carlos, who's finally succeeded in getting a cab.

"You should have an affair with a rich married man!" Maya shouts out to me loudly enough for both Carlos and the cabdriver to hear, before she tosses her hair and goes back inside Tarts to meet up with Jay, who's neither rich nor married—so much for following her own advice.

Carlos holds the cab door open for me. Neither he nor I comment on Maya's outcry, although the cabdriver, a blond kid with a baseball cap on backwards, gives me a private smile in the dashboard mirror as I step inside, and despite myself, I smile back. He's pretty cute, too, probably another struggling actor or singer moonlighting as a cabbie—and, very possibly, judging by his inviting smile, another candidate for an extramarital fling for me. But no, if I'm going to have one, it's going to be tonight, with Carlos. Definitely. I stop smiling at the driver. No point in encouraging him.

Meanwhile, Carlos and I are suddenly very tense with each other. I slide all the way to one side of the seat. He slides all the way to the other. We don't say a word to each other during the cab ride uptown. He looks out the window on his side of the cab. I look out the window on my side. When we stop for a light somewhere near Houston Street, I witness what looks like a drug deal taking place between one man, dressed in a leather jacket and skintight jeans, and a second man carrying a fancy-looking cane and wearing a wide-brimmed hat.

I don't know whether Carlos is witnessing similar sights from his side, but I do know that the tension between us is getting thicker by the minute. It's now as thick as my head must have been ever to have believed, even for one moment, that George and Nicole Burden were working late together, night after night. This thought makes me feel glad that there's so much sexual tension between me and Carlos tonight. I remember how much I loved this kind of sexual tension in my single days. Sometimes it was more fun than the actual sex that followed it, sadly.

The driver pulls up in front of Lydia's building.

We don't speak during the elevator ride. Carlos opens the door to Lydia's apartment. We seem, though, to be communicating in some way other than speech. Together, side by side, we head directly into Lydia's small, dark bedroom. Flaca follows us.

Carlos sits on the unmade bed. He removes his mirrored sunglasses.

I'm not quite ready to join him on the bed. Deliberately, I sit across the room, sinking into a black director's chair. Flaca climbs, with great effort, onto the top of Lydia's cluttered bureau.

The three of us are silent.

I close my eyes, picturing how our lovemaking will begin. Carlos will rise from the bed. He'll come to me. Gently, he'll wrap his arms around me. I'll lift my face up toward his. He'll sink to his knees. Our lips will meet. And then, we're "gonna do it," as Maya and I used to say when we were kids. "Look, Maya, I bet they're gonna go home and do it!" I'd whisper, feeling thrilled, pointing to some older teenage couple making out on a bench in Bronx Park.

No, there's no reason for me to wait for Carlos to start. I open my eyes. I rise. I walk to the bed, where he's sitting, his back against the wall, watching me. I lean over him and I wrap my arms around him. I sink onto the bed next to him, and I kiss him. A lusty kiss. He kisses me back, and I lean into him. His arms envelop me. I remember the first moments of first nights like this so well. I sigh. I lean my head back and Carlos strokes my neck. And then I yawn. Loudly. Carlos looks confused. And I'm embarrassed. But I'm also sleepy. Very, very sleepy. All of a sudden, sleep is the only thing that I want to do all the way. I yawn a second time, even more loudly. This yawn feels delicious, like all of my favorite ice-cream flavors combined. I no longer feel even slightly devilish from the vodka; I feel totally wiped out.

Carlos takes my chin in his hand and lifts my face toward his. "Listen," he says excitedly, and his voice is brimming with sexual innuendo, "don't fall asleep on me now. I'm going to go get us something. But I'll be right back." In my sleepy haze, I suspect he's talking about getting us some condoms, which may not be the most romantic thing in the world, but it's definitely a wise and safe thing to do. The next thing I know, he's shaking me awake. He sits me up. I feel loose and limp, like one of Lydia's Raggedy Ann dolls.

He wraps my hand around a large mug of coffee. "Drink this," he says.

I sip the coffee. It's vile.

"Here's my proposition," he says.

This is it. He's going to ask me to do it. I have to wake up. And I have to decide.

Carlos is sitting across from me in the director's chair, slurping noisily at his own mug of coffee. I wonder whether his coffee tastes as bad as mine, or whether he deliberately made mine vile to keep me awake. "Let's combine forces," he says enthusiastically.

What a strange way to describe sex. _Combine forces_ is even less erotic than _doing it._

"Let's work together," he says. "On _Hard-Boiled._ I need your help."

At first I wonder if he's teasing me, trying to keep me awake by getting on my nerves. But he appears absolutely serious. And I feel torn between laughing and crying, between feeling relieved that I don't have to make a decision about sleeping with him tonight and insulted that he's so involved in his art that—at least for the moment—he's more interested in that than in my body, despite our lusty kisses. And I still can't shake off this drowsiness.

He speaks rapidly. "I just haven't been able to hit it right, to figure out exactly how to say what I want to say in _Hard-Boiled._ But I've been thinking. About both of us feeling betrayed and lovesick. And about some of the things you've talked about—like your journal therapy, and your ambivalence about having a baby, and the women in the locker room...." He looks really excited now. "And I'm convinced that what I need for this piece is a woman's point of view. _Your_ point of view."

I force myself to sip the coffee again. I grimace. "Forget it, Carlos. I'm no artist." My voice is slow and sleepy.

"Are you sure?" he asks intensely.

I nod. "Yes, I'm sure. I can't draw. I can't sing. I can't dance. I get anxiety attacks when I try to write. So what kind of artist could I possibly be?" I feel as though I'm speaking through layers of fog, as though my voice is unintelligible. I glance over at Flaca. She also looks sleepy now.

"I've got a nose for artists," Carlos says insistently. "I can sniff them out. Put me in a room filled with undertakers, and I'll sniff out the one who's secretly writing a novel. Sometimes it's a curse. But, anyway, you've got the smell."

"No, I don't. That's Lydia's smell. It's all over the apartment," I say sleepily.

"Just listen to me, okay? Here's my idea for *Hard-Boiled*. The detective—*our* detective, I mean—will be a dame." He pauses, and adds politely, "A woman."

I shake my head again, and the fog finally begins to lift. I'm waking up. Maybe I'm also sobering up. I blink a few times, pushing my hair out of my eyes. "Forget it, Carlos. Dame or woman, honestly, it doesn't matter, because I don't have a creative bone in my body. Do you understand? I can recognize interesting, innovative, out-of-the-mainstream work, and I love and value the arts with all my heart and soul, and I'm a good organizer. And that's why I'm good at my job at TAG. But that's it! That's *all* I am." There, now he's gotten me completely overwrought. But at least he'll get the message loud and clear. He'll back off. To my surprise, though, instead of backing off, he comes over to the bed and sits down next to me. I wonder whether he's going to come on to me again. I move away. I'm no longer feeling quite as warmly toward him, although I'm still feeling somewhat aroused.

He moves closer. He's so close that he's practically on top of me. "See," he says, suddenly sounding like Humphrey Bogart, "our dame, I mean, woman detective is on the trail of someone who's been knocking off the female members of this really snazzy Park Avenue health club! One by one, these ladies are being murdered in the locker room. So one of these ladies, a rich broad in a fur coat, thinks she's going to be next. And she hires our dame detective to find the killer before she ends up looking like a slab of rich meat on a cement block in the morgue."

I lean back, further away from him. He leans forward. "And

the journal?" I ask. "How does journal-keeping fit into it?" Despite myself, I'm growing a little curious about the plot of _Hard-Boiled_, not that I would ever dream of working on it with him.

"Our dame detective is a literary dame, see," Carlos answers, still doing his Humphrey Bogart imitation, and placing his hand on my knee. He's obviously no longer worried that I might take offense at the word _dame_, and he's still interested in my body, after all. "She reads books," he goes on, "and she keeps this journal. She records clues in it. And her feelings, too."

"And the lovesickness? Where does that come in?" I try to ignore his hand, which feels warm. My heart is pounding.

"Our dame's always been a loner. But recently she got soft. She allowed some guy to get inside her skin. But he turned out to be a low-down, two-timing double-crosser." He moves his hand slightly higher.

"So now she's even tougher and more hard-boiled than she was before, right?" My voice sounds low and husky, and I still refuse to allow my glance to stray to his hand.

"Right."

"What about the baby issue? Where does that fit in?" My voice is now way down in the Tallulah Bankhead range.

He increases the pressure of his hand on my knee. "She's a sensitive dame, see, and sometimes she wishes that she'd settled down and gotten married and had lots of children like all the other girls in her hometown. But other times she's one hundred percent happy that she became a tough cookie detective instead." His voice—still in Bogie mode—is also deeper and huskier than usual.

I close my eyes for a moment: This dame detective is starting to come to life for me. I can picture exactly what she looks like: She's tall. Wiry and sexy. Long, wavy brown hair, swept over one eye, in a Veronica Lake style, just like mine. She wears a tan trench coat. She has a tendency to slouch in doorways. Her perfume smells like a smoking gun. "Her name," I say, sounding now

like a very breathless Talullah Bankhead, "could be Phyllis Marlowe. Or Sammi Spade."

Carlos grins. "And remember, Babette," he says, now rubbing
his hand more aggressively up and down my thigh, "this isn't con-
ventional stuff." He sounds breathless too. "Our dame detective is
also slightly frustrated—like you."

I wonder whether he means sexually frustrated, the way I'm
feeling at this moment, as I sit here, unsure whether to lunge at
him or not. I look directly into his eyes, and I see a combination of
sexual lust and artistic fanaticism, which only increases my own
frustration.

He continues. "She's frustrated because, like you, she doesn't
feel that she's yet achieved her full potential in life." He wraps his
leg over mine. I can hardly breathe. "So she's decided to write a
TV pilot called *Hard-Boiled*," he goes on, speaking even more
rapidly and breathlessly, "which is, naturally, based on her own
life, and she wants this really kooky performance artist, sort of like
Lydia, to play the lead role." He stares at me, and I look away. I
don't fully understand whether his seductiveness is aimed at getting me into bed with him, or into becoming his collaborator on
Hard-Boiled. Or both. "But this performance artist," he says, "has
all these ideas of her own—like she wants the story to be told out
of time sequence, and she wants her voice to be electronically
manipulated, and she wants the TV show's theme music to be
microtonal...."

I haven't the vaguest idea what *microtonal* means, but still, I
know—and he knows that I know—that I'm hooked. "Okay,
Carlos. I'll do it." I mean only the collaboration part, though, not
the sex. I hope that he understands this.

"That's great, Babette," Carlos says, smiling. "And by the way,"
he wraps his leg tighter around mine, "I'd also like to make love
with you tonight." He takes my hand and rubs my palm across his
lips. His lips are surprisingly—and invitingly—soft and warm.

I shiver with both lust and fear. I would love to make love with him. But I can't. I just can't. Agreeing to write a play, considering I have acute writing anxiety, is enough turmoil for one night. I can't believe that I—lusty, aggressive Babette Bliss—have become what the boys back in the Bronx used to call a "cockteaser." Well, it isn't my fault. It's George's. He's turned my life upside down; he's the one who's got me acting "a little bit crazy" all the time. "Carlos, I can't," I manage to say. "I just can't."

He sighs and lets go of my hand. He waits a minute, though, before unwrapping his leg from mine, as though he's waiting for me to change my mind. Finally, he sighs again and disentangles himself.

"I understand, Babette," he says. "But if you change your mind…" He stands, still looking at me hopefully.

I look over at Flaca instead, who's beginning to snore softly from her position on top of Lydia's bureau. I keep staring at her, until I hear Carlos leave the room. And then, fully clothed, using Flaca as my role model, I will myself to fall asleep.

20

The Music Library at Lincoln Center is airy and quiet. Just being around all of these erudite-looking composer types makes me want to burst into song, if only the library rules didn't forbid it, and if only I had a decent voice.

I'm here researching microtonal music for *Hard-Boiled*, which Carlos and I have begun working on. He's still giving me an occasional seductive, heavy-lidded glance, but at least he's dropped all overt references to us becoming lovers. I'm grateful that he has, even though his heavy-lidded glances are very appealing, and I'm still indulging in an occasional fantasy about his tender-but-virile lovemaking. But I've definitely decided that my first extramarital affair shouldn't be with my artistic collaborator, no matter how attractive he is—no mixing of business with pleasure. Despite my profound state of ambivalence these days, that's one thing I'm sure of.

What I'm less sure of is whether I'm really ready to begin a career as a playwright. But I seem to be doing it, ready or not. I've just learned, for instance, that microtonal music is music that uses "extremely small divisions of a scale." Meaning that it always sounds out of tune. Which seems appropriate, since my own life seems so out of tune these days.

And another thing I'm not at all sure about is how in the world I'll be able to support myself if I become a divorceé _and_ a cutting edge playwright, simultaneously.

In the meantime, though, I'm suppressing my fears, and I'm trying, instead, to dig up names of some musicians who play microtonal music. New York isn't exactly crawling with them. For one thing, playing out-of-tune songs on bizarre-looking instruments is a lot less lucrative than playing Frank Sinatra songs at weddings. And for another, it doesn't usually lead to a permanent gig at the Philharmonic. Still, my research has turned up the curious fact that, somewhere in New Jersey, there exists something called The Microtonal Music Collective; I can't help but imagining its members as a group of bearded fanatics who wear white robes, rope-soled sandals, and eat only berries.

After I copy down the collective's address, I return the various music journals I've been reading to the librarian at the desk. With her curly red hair and thick eyeglasses, she reminds me of an intellectual version of Shara-Rose, with whom I've negotiated a truce over the debacle at Tarts. I called her the next morning. "Listen, it's okay that you came to hear me sing," she said. "After all, I can't tell you what to do. But just don't ever come again." "Okay," I agreed, deciding not to point out to that she'd just contradicted herself within seconds by telling me exactly what to do. Instead, I told her about what had happened back at Lydia's afterward. She seemed pleased that I'd said no to Carlos about sex. "I don't think you're _quite_ ready for a serious fling, Babette, until you take care of your own shit, pardon my French," was how she'd put it. She _had_ agreed, though, that he's "very cute in a sort of pseudo-academic way." But she seemed even more pleased about my working on _Hard-Boiled_. "That's _great_, Babette," she'd shouted into the phone, so loudly I had to move it a few inches away from my ear. "You're *writing!*" Although she didn't know what microtonal music was, either.

The Music Library is on the third floor. I ride down to the lobby, sharing the elevator with a painfully thin woman wearing a leotard top and ankle-length jersey skirt; she's practicing her ballet positions. Since she's not at all self-conscious about dancing in the elevator, I indulge my desire to sing. Very, very softly, under my breath, I sing Beatle George's melancholy song "When We Was Fab." He, of course, is reminiscing about the long-lost heyday of the Beatles. I, on the other hand, am reminiscing about the long-lost heyday of my marriage. When the elevator lands, the woman gracefully pirouettes out, while I exit slowly, still singing softly, and taking my time as I walk through the lobby.

I stop singing when I step outside, and I head back to Lydia's, but instead of walking down Ninth, I detour and walk west, until I find myself standing on the corner of 57th and Tenth. TAG's corner. I look up at TAG's window, hoping that nobody sees me. My heart is pounding, and I feel guilty and paranoid: a criminal returning to the scene of the crime. I go so far as to wipe my brow and look over my shoulder. As though I've got no choice, I find myself entering the five-story brick building and climbing the three flights of stairs to TAG.

On the third-floor landing, I hesitate. I picture TAG the way it looked when I last saw it. I hope that Jay hasn't allowed Maya to come in and redecorate. TAG rents the entire third floor. There's a cramped office, with peeling walls, that Jay and I share. And a tiny dressing room, with a peeling ceiling, for the performers. And a small kitchen, with a peeling ceiling *and* peeling walls, where Jay and I make coffee all day long, and where the health-conscious, calorie-counting performers keep their containers of low-calorie yogurt and their carrot sticks. There are also, of course, the two theaters. Both of which Jay and I somehow always have managed to keep in decent shape so that nothing, knock on wood, is peeling. And we've managed to do this despite the landlord, Mr. Lombardo, who's owned the building for twenty-seven years and who has never, to my knowledge, put a single cent into maintenance. One of the theaters is so small that when twenty-five people are in the audience it feels crowded. But the other theater, Jay's pride and joy, holds about a hundred and fifty people.

Tentatively, I open the door to the office. I stand in the doorway, and the first thing I notice is that the office looks completely familiar, exactly the way it always looked, with none of Maya's pink gewgaws in sight. The second thing I notice is Jay, who's wearing one of his baggy checkered jackets. He's sitting on top of his desk, pushing his sliding eyeglasses up, and dialing the phone. This is also a completely familiar sight, since Jay spends most of his life wearing baggy jackets, adjusting his sliding eyeglasses, and doing business on the phone. I no longer feel guilty or paranoid. I feel relieved. And reassured and comforted by the familiarity of the office, and Jay.

I sense that Jay has the urge to smile when he sees me. I also sense that the urge passes quickly. Instead, without smiling, he looks at his watch. "The meeting is about to start," he says, sounding uncharacteristically mysterious and Kafka-esque. "You're just in time." He removes his finger from the dial, but doesn't let go of the receiver. "Go into the small theater and join the rest of them," he adds, without further explanation. He's not behaving at all like himself. He resumes dialing the phone, clearly dismissing me.

I back out the door, feeling much less comfortable. I'm breathing rapidly and starting to sweat. But I do as I'm told. I enter the small theater, where a few of the other tenants in the building are sitting on metal folding chairs in a circle on the stage. They all look hot and sweaty, which must mean that the air-conditioner is broken again, and that Jay can't afford to have it fixed. It also means that they'll all probably assume I'm sweating for the same reasons they are, instead of because I'm feeling so guilty.

Doreen Cioffi, the Director of FemmeDance, the all-woman modern dance troupe on the fifth floor, is the first to spot me. "Babette," she shouts out heartily, wiping her neck with a large red-and-black checkered handkerchief, "it's good to see you. Come, pull up a chair. We're working out the last-minute arrangements for the demonstration next week." Doreen is broad-shouldered and tall, with jet-black hair that falls to her waist.

Wiping my brow and attempting an innocent, casual smile, I climb the steps to the stage and, as jauntily as I can, I drag over a metal chair for myself from the corner.

I sit next to Doreen, trying to look calm, upbeat, and eager to discuss the demonstration.

"You've been on vacation, right?" Doreen asks.

I nod, relieved that she doesn't seem to notice anything out of the ordinary about my behavior. I do hope, though, that she isn't about to ask me *how* I've been spending my summer vacation. I don't want to have to admit that I've spent it one block away, moping on 56th Street. Luckily, she doesn't ask me, and the meeting resumes.

"I've contacted all the TV stations about the demonstration—network and cable," Doreen announces.

Karl Ranger is as small and narrow as Doreen is tall and broad. He's about five three, and fine-boned. He owns *Tresses on Tenth*, a small hair salon on the second floor. He speaks softly, in the gentle Mississippi drawl he hasn't lost despite ten years in Manhattan. "I keep bugging the radio stations," he runs his fingers through his finely textured auburn hair, "and I think I've stirred up some interest."

Pearl Green is sitting next to Karl, listening seriously to him. She's a novelist who has a studio on the first floor. Pearl is divorced, with three children and an ailing mother all living at home with her. She needs, as she puts it, "a room of my own." She speaks in her very sober manner. "Yes, we will get some media attention. But I'm not convinced that it will be sympathetic." Pearl always dresses in dark-colored, conservative suits, and her manner is stiff, but I don't blame her one bit. I have a hunch that her home life isn't exactly the stuff of TV sitcoms.

Doreen wipes her neck again with the checkered handkerchief. "I called Mr. Lombardo the other day," she says.

We all stare at her. Since Mr. Lombardo, who's never been a great landlord to begin with, has committed the ultimate act of betrayal by selling the building to Acme Developers when all of our leases were up, without even giving us warning, none of us are his biggest fans right now.

Doreen continues, tossing her thick bangs out of her eyes. "I woke him during his afternoon nap. But I didn't care." She's so animated now that her booming voice is echoing throughout the tiny theater. "I said to him, 'Mr. Lombardo, you're throwing us all out into the street. We can't afford to rent elsewhere. There's no space for artists in New York any longer. What you've done—selling us off like cattle—is immoral!'"

Karl stares at her in awe. "You really said that to him? _Immoral?_" His soft voice is incredulous.

Doreen nods fiercely. "Yes, I said it. And he said..." and she launches into a booming imitation of his old-world Italian accent—which, I guess, being Italian herself and having grown up in South Philly, she does brilliantly—"'Doreen, Doreen, I've got three grandchildren in college, and my wife, she wants to move to a nice condo in Florida. Don't give me this immoral crap! You're a dancer, Doreen. So dance. Who's stopping you?'"

We're all silent. The issues are complicated. None of us wants to feel responsible for depriving Mr. Lombardo's grandchildren of their college education, or Mrs. Lombardo of the comforts of Florida in her golden years. Mr. Lombardo owns just a few small buildings; he's no big-time slumlord.

"Still," Pearl says seriously, crossing her sturdy legs and smoothing her navy blue skirt, "he easily could have sold the building for a little less money, to a buyer who didn't want to tear it down, who wanted to preserve it, to make improvements. Which," she adds darkly, "he certainly never did. And his grandchildren and wife would still be sitting pretty. That would have been moral."

Karl frowns. "All I know is," he speaks slowly and softly, as always, but with a great passion, "if I lose this space, I'm going to give up trying to make a go of my own business. There's no place for small businesses in this city. If I'm lucky, I'll find a job cutting hair in one of those ostentatious Columbus Avenue shops.... If I'm not lucky," he sighs and rests his hand on his forehead, as though he's getting a headache, "I'll have to go back to my people in Mississippi." He looks depressed.

Jay is climbing the stage to join us. He pulls up a chair next to Pearl. "Sarah will be here soon," he announces, sounding like himself again: totally manic and tense. This convinces me that his cool performance earlier was deliberate, for my benefit, to unnerve me. "Sarah's been on the phone night and day," he continues, "talking to newspapers and magazines, and she's lined up a few interviews." He looks pointedly at me. "So you see, Babette, a lot has been going on in your absence."

I wonder if Jay will ever stop trying to make me feel guilty for daring to take time off this summer. But now I've got something else, or should I say, some*one* else, on my mind, besides guilt: Nicole Burden's little cousin Sarah.

21

Moments later, Sarah Burden climbs the steps leading to the stage. She isn't sweating at all, I notice. She's younger than Nicole, of course. And shorter. More on the cute side than the beautiful. But the sculpted, aristocratic features are very similar. She's definitely a blood relative. Or, given the ruthlessness of Grandpa Abner and cousin Nicole, perhaps a blood*less* relative would be more accurate.

Unlike cousin Nicole, her blond hair is cut in a short, perky bob. She's wearing a lavender-colored cotton pullover sweater, and a knee-length beige skirt. The perfect shoes for this outfit would be a pair of shiny penny loafers with tassels. But the Burden females are always filled with surprises, and Sarah is wearing lavender Fuck-Me shoes instead.

Nodding hello to everyone, she pulls up a chair next to Jay. The meeting continues, but now things are a blur for me. I no longer pay any attention to what's being said about the demonstration, although I can see that Sarah is animated and talkative, and that Doreen, Karl, and Pearl all like her.

Abruptly, the meeting ends. At least it feels abrupt to me, but then, I've been so completely immersed in my thoughts about little cousin Sarah, who, it seems to me, has a hell of a lot of nerve to be sitting here in the same space as I am, inhaling the same air as I am. TAG's air, no less. But Doreen, Karl, and Pearl are all standing up, pushing back their chairs, saying *Ciao* to one another, and heading back to their own studios. Which means that Jay, Sarah, and I are alone together. "Babette," Jay says, finally having the decency to look uncomfortable, "meet Sarah."

"Hi," Sarah smiles widely, directly at me, and I note, for the first time, what really separates perky little Sarah from elegant, cool Nicole. It's Sarah's smile, which reveals a large space between her front teeth. Ordinarily, I find gap-toothed smiles very endearing. But not today.

"It's a pleasure to meet you," Sarah says. "I've heard so much about you."

Wondering if Nicole and Sarah have frequent tête-à-têtes to discuss me, I respond icily, "And just what have you heard about me?" Sorry, Sarah: The stoical, long-suffering wife who behaves graciously not only to her husband's mistress, but to her husband's mistress's cousin as well, is one role I'm determined not to play.

She has the nerve to feign surprise at my icy demeanor and my question. "I've heard that...you've done great things...for TAG," she answers uncertainly.

Before Sarah and I can say anything more to each other, Jay hastily pushes his sliding eyeglasses up, rises from his chair in typical manic fashion, and without a word, as though he's just remembered that his apartment is on fire, bounds down the steps of the stage and out the theater.

Perky Sarah, who appeared perfectly cool throughout the meeting despite the heat, is finally starting to sweat. Sitting awkwardly on stage together like this, we might be two actresses about to read for an audition. Except that someone forgot to hand us our scripts.

"So listen, Sarah," I say, desperate to say something, anything, to let her know that despite our mutual connection to TAG, I want nothing to do with her, or with any other Burden, for that matter, "you might have had the decency not to come to work here." My voice is throbbing with emotion. I'm starting to get a headache.

"May I ask why?"

I hear two distinct things in her voice. One is that she's young, nervous, and a bit unsure of herself. The other is that, deep down, she's also strong-willed and confident, which is what, undoubtedly, has allowed her to come to TAG's aid with such fervor. Ordinarily I would find the combination of these two traits likeable. But again, not today. I also resent her because her role as the sweet young ingenue is a lot easier to play than my role as the betrayed wife, especially since I'm so determined to play against type. There really aren't a whole lot of positive role models out there for me. "Your cousin…" I begin, "…and my husband…" This feels awkward and absurd: my spelling out for her what she already knows. I could really use a director to step in and tell me exactly what to say, and how to say it.

"Yes?" Sarah Burden asks, her eyes bright and curious. She's too damned good in this ingenue role. She must have been a theater major back at Sarah Lawrence. I take a quick peek at her lavender shoes, which are anything but sweet and innocent. "Oh, come on," I say impatiently, "don't try to tell me you don't know."

She smiles her gap-toothed smile. "I don't."

I finally have it. I feel inspired. I'll model myself after Phillipa Marlowe, avant-garde, hard-boiled female detective. "Your cousin and my husband," I bark, "have been screwing!" There, I've said it, tough and brassy, and it's a relief, actually, to come right out and say it like that. Right to the face of a Burden.

Sarah swivels her head and looks around the theater, maybe looking for an escape route. Or maybe she's also looking for a director to step in and help her out.

Dramatically, still in my Phillipa Marlow role, I rise, pushing my chair back so violently it makes a loud screech.

She rises, too. "Honestly," she says, looking imploringly at me, "I didn't know. I mean, nobody said a word to me. Not Nicole. Not Jay. All I knew was that your husband is a lawyer with Granddaddy's firm, and that he and Nicole work together, and that you were generous enough to recommend me to Jay. And that I care about TAG. Honestly."

Despite myself, I'm tempted to believe her. "Next you'll tell me that those," I point to the lavender shoes, "are Nicole's shoes, and not yours."

Confused, she looks down at her shoes. She makes a face. "They are a bit much, aren't they? I bought them when I came to work here. I thought they'd make me look more sophisticated." Furtively, she looks around the theater again, before whispering, "At school we used to call shoes like this Fuck-Me shoes."

To my surprise, I find myself smiling. And I begin to worry: If I spend too much time around this girl, I could learn to like her. Which means I have to leave immediately.

22

When I open the door to Jay's office, I expect to find him sitting on top of his desk, fiddling with his sliding eyeglasses and speaking on the phone. He *is* sitting on top of his desk, and he is fiddling with his sliding eyeglasses. But he isn't on the phone. Instead, right there in front of me, he's chatting away with George and Maya.

I stand in the doorway, staring. Maya is sitting in Jay's chair; George is sitting on top of my desk. I ignore Maya, and I focus on George. What chutzpah. What gall. Sitting on *my* desk. This would be the perfect moment in a hard-boiled mystery to whip out my gun and splatter the office with bullets. The truth, however, is that seeing George like that, sitting there in his neat, tailored pin-striped suit—such a contrast to the crumpled Jay—I feel something besides anger. Something tender. Well, we *are* still married. Still husband and wife. Still bound in some way, despite the fact that he's betrayed me with an Ice Queen in Fuck-Me shoes, and also that I won't speak to him.

Hesitantly, George smiles at me. "Babette," he says, "Jay told me that you'd stopped by. I'm happy to see you."

I remain in the doorway. "What," I ask Jay, "is *he* doing here?"

Jay has the decency to look uncomfortable. "He's answering some legal questions for me."

"That's right, that's what he's doing," George says, getting right into the spirit of discussing himself in the third person. "Also," he goes on, "he was hoping that you'd drop by."

"As it turns out," Jay says, glancing at his watch, with evident relief in his voice, "Maya and I have to race across town to pick Alex up from school. She's going to perform the latest version of *Alex Does It* for us. She's gotten so into it, she's even added some kind of music."

For one eerie moment, I wonder whether Alex, too, has discovered microtonal music. For her sake, I hope not; I hope her tastes are going to run more to the mainstream—like the score of *Cats*—so that one day she'll be able to earn big bucks and not have to drive taxis on the side and depend on tiny grants from struggling arts organizations in order to survive. I also hope that she'll soon have her chance to perform *Alex Does It* at TAG, since it obviously means a lot to her. But of course, none of that is my immediate concern. My immediate concern is George's presence.

Maya rises regally. "Babette, may I speak to you privately for a moment, please?"

After her last two "private talks" with me—at the Quickie-Weight-Loss meeting and in the doorway of Tarts—I'm not very much in the mood. Still, against my better judgment, I follow her out into the hallway. She closes the door, and begins to speak in a melodramatic stage whisper. "You know, you *are* acting a little bit crazy concerning George."

"Maya, I am not," I find myself stage whispering back. "And I'm also getting sick and tired of hearing you say that I am! I just happen to be in the process of *thinking deeply* about my life. And that takes time. It can't be rushed. I'm doing a lot of very _positive_ things, actually, a lot of very _noncrazy_ things. I'm doing journal therapy, writing a play, eating ice cream, swimming at my health club. I'm even flirting with men. What more can be expected of me?"

"Babette, you're making much too much of all this. So George fell in love with another woman for a while—it happens."

Again, she's managed to say absolutely the wrong thing. I haven't allowed myself, not really, to believe that George _loved_— or perhaps even still _loves_—Nicole Burden. Well, sometimes, in my _very worst_ fantasies, I do imagine him telling her that he _loves, loves, loves_ her, far more than he'd ever loved that pushy Jewish girl from the Bronx with her avant-garde, nonlucrative taste in theater. But most of the time I don't allow my worst fantasies to take over. Instead, I indulge in more middle-of-the-road fantasies, in which it's merely lust—never _love, love, love_—that drives him into her arms, lust fired up by the temptation of those bright red Fuck-Me shoes and those expensive mammoth fur coats. I also assume there's some ambition mixed in with the lust, since George wouldn't mind, I know, becoming a full partner in the firm of Burden, Lawrence, Shapiro, and O'Reilly. I don't respond to what Maya has said, though. I don't want her to see how much this hurts—and scares—me.

She goes on, leaning forward, warming to her subject, her stage whisper growing louder and more impassioned. "Men fool around. It's biological. Women are inclined to be monogamous and men aren't. You can't fight nature."

Now she's gotten me incredibly angry, so I can't focus so much on my hurt and fear, which is a good thing, I suppose. I give up on the stage whispering, not caring any longer if my voice does carry through the closed door. "That's ridiculous, Maya! As though women don't have desires? That's exactly the kind of 1950s bull-shit, _retro_ comment that's designed to keep women barefoot, preg-nant, and in the kitchen! That comment makes me sick!"

Maya sighs, as though I'm hopeless.

"Forget it, Maya. You wouldn't understand. But maybe you can understand this. I'm *hurt*. Honestly. My feelings are hurt. Can't you understand that? Remember when Ricky dumped you for that phoney surfer babe, Cupcake, back in high school? You were hurt, right? Remember when your ex-husband left you for a nineteen-year-old showroom model with 40-D breast implants? It hurt, right?" It seems inexplicable to me that Maya, who wept for years over Merv's infidelities, can't seem to fathom that I, too, am feeling rejected.

She shrugs. "Babette, nobody's dumping you. You're the one doing the dumping. And besides, you're totally oversensitive. Remember when Mrs. Whitehawk told you that you'd put all the semicolons in the wrong places in your paper on Herman Melville, remember how you cried every night for a week?"

At the mention of the terrifying Mrs. Whitehawk, I decide to end the conversation. "I'm going back inside. And you should go pick Alex up from school before she starts to feel abandoned. Oh, and tell her—from me—not to worry in advance what the critics will say about *Alex Does It*. Tell her to be true to her own muse, lucrative or not." I turn on my heel before Maya can say anything else.

As soon as I'm inside, Jay makes a big production of looking at his watch again, jumping up from his desk, and racing out into the hallway to meet up with Maya. And then they're gone.

George and I are alone. Once again, I could use the help of a good script and a good director. I'm not even sure why I'm back in Jay's office. But I feel stuck, my feet planted to the floor. In the meantime, I'll just continue to wing it à la Phillipa Marlowe.

"Babette," George says softly, "there are so many things I'd like to say to you. So many things I'd like to explain."

There's something so reasonable-sounding about his voice. So sane. So sensible. Isn't it a wife's obligation to listen to her husband?

"What I did, there are no excuses for," he goes on. "Absolutely none. I know that. Do you think I don't know that?"

I have the right, I remind myself, to remain silent. But the sight of him perched on my desk compels me somehow, despite my resolve, to respond. "Neither your motives, nor your degree of self-awareness, are my concern." I can't believe I've just given in and spoken to him. To my surprise, though, my voice sounds cool, distanced, and unemotional, despite my inner turmoil. I cross the room and sit on top of Jay's desk.

"But," George says earnestly, "if we're going to save our marriage, those things have to become your concerns. _Our_ concerns. We need to discuss all of that. And..." he hesitates, "...whether something _was_ wrong in our relationship. Something neither of us was aware of. It's possible." He shrugs. "On the other hand, it may be a simple story of an Iowan farmboy who made it a little too big in the big city, and who didn't know how to handle it."

"Please, spare me the pop psychology." I'm impressed with myself: on the outside, as hard as stone; on the inside, as soft as melting ice cream. I look away, lest my little facade crack, and the melting ice cream come pouring through.

"The thing is," he says, "I've found someone."

I stare at him. I can't believe my ears. First he tells me that he wants to save the marriage. And now, less than a minute later, he's telling me that he's found someone else. Does he think that the way to save our marriage is to let me know in advance from now on when he's found a lover?

"Through Shara-Rose," he adds.

This is too much. My shrink is pimping for my husband. I indulge in a fantasy: I'll set fire to Tarts the next time Mild Neurosis plays there.

"His name," George says, "is Dr. First."

I understand. Dr. First is a therapist. Not a lover. I allow myself one private and silent moment of relief. Then, in as cool and patronizing a voice as I can muster, I say, "You're still clinging to this ridiculous idea about couple therapy, aren't you? Still thinking that all we need to do is have a loving, sincere chat in some shrink's office, and all will be well?" Maybe, after all, I really do have what it takes to make it as an actress. With my Veronica Lake hairdo, I could move to Hollywood, buy a house with a heart-shaped swimming pool, and say a permanent farewell to George.

George replies in the reasonable, convincing tones of a good lawyer. "I'm not suggesting that psychotherapy is the answer to all the world's ills, but I am suggesting that it might provide us with an objective forum in which to begin to communicate reasonably about the various events that have occurred."

Another fantasy: I gather all the money-making professionals of our society, the lawyers, shrinks, landlords, etc., and send them into outer space where they can start their own planet, on which everyone speaks only legalese and psychobabble. And the rest of us would be left in peace on earth, and we'd also start saving money, without their inflated fees and monthly bills.

"Just think about it, okay?" he asks. "I've called Dr. First, and I've explained our situation. He's willing to see us. So all I'm asking is for you to call me and let me know if you change your mind." He slaps his hands on his thighs. "But I won't take up any more of your time. I'm sure you're busy, now that you're back at TAG."

"I'm not exactly back. I'm only here due to mysterious circumstances beyond my control."

"You know, I've been feeling exactly the same way." He smiles as though I've just made a joke.

"I wasn't joking." But I'm smiling too. "After all," I say, now feeling compelled to make a joke despite myself, "wasn't it Dashiel Hammett who said, 'Life's a bitch, and then you die'?" "No," he says, still smiling, "that was Raymond Chandler. Dashiel Hammett said, 'Life's a *beach*, and then you die.'"

We sit silently for a minute, grinning like idiots at each other.

And I wonder what it would take on my part to forgive this man, my husband, with whom I have this rapport? A snap of my fingers, a blink of my eye? Except that I can't seem to figure out where forgiveness ends and masochism begins. How many women forgive and forgive, time after time, accepting their husbands' lying and philandering, because they're too frightened to be alone? Or because they think—like Maya—that it's all about biology, and that biology is destiny? I stop smiling. Still, sometimes I wonder whether I'm more angry than hurt. Maybe I'm really angry because I turned down all those gorgeous actors who'd come on to me over the years at TAG. Also, I have to ask myself, how much of this is about my pride, and how much about real sorrow? I'm being very hard on myself, true, but could Maya be right? Am I still that oversensitive girl who cried for days over Mrs. Whitehawk's brutal accusations about my semicolons? Then again, I'm not absolutely certain I _do_ believe that things are over between George and Nicole. Why _should_ I believe him? The man's a proven liar! _Oh, what a tangled web we weave_, I think—another old phrase that seems quite to the point.

"Well," he sighs, his own smile fading, "I've got to get back to work."

"Working away on some new case with Nicole, I presume," I say nastily.

He looks down. "No. Just so you know...Nicole..." and he sounds truly miserable speaking her name to me, "is...away. She's not at the office these days."

"Nicole's whereabouts are of no concern to me." But of course I do wonder where she is. Maybe she's off on a worldwide shopping spree, searching every corner of the earth for the perfect pair of Fuck-Me shoes. "And don't expect me to see this Dr. First with you. Or Dr. Second, or Dr. Third, for that matter. Or even," I add pleasantly, "Dr. Strangelove."

"What about Dr. Jekyll?" he asks, smiling again.

I can't stop myself: "I'd rather hide." Now I'm smiling again, too. It's catching.

He slides easily off the desk. "Listen," he says seriously, standing in front of me, staring at me intensely, "I miss you."

I'm no longer smiling. And neither is he. I have the feeling he's about to burst into yet another Beatles song. If he does, I'll scream.

He doesn't sing, though. He leaves, without turning around to look at me. And for the first time, I have a really strong urge to get back to Lydia's and do some journal therapy in earnest. I wait a few minutes to be sure that George has had plenty of time to get clear of the building. And then I fly down the steps and out into the street. On the corner of 57th and Ninth, I spot Sarah Burden, looking precariously balanced in her lavender Fuck-Me shoes, handing out change to a couple of homeless people. I nod at her, but before she can say anything, I walk on.

23

Shara-Rose is sitting perfectly still in her black leather armchair. I'm sitting on her sofa, in a blue tank top and a pair of really short dungaree shorts, which I confess I've been wearing a lot these days, because I'm enjoying watching Carlos staring at my legs with desire while I walk around Lydia's apartment. Right now, however, I wish I weren't wearing them, because the leather of Shara-Rose's sofa is sticking to my bare thighs.

Shara-Rose appears distracted, as though she's not really here with me. I can't put my finger on how I know this, but I know that she's thinking about other things besides my neuroses. And it's very frustrating, because I'm particularly excited about our session today: I want to read yesterday's journal entry aloud to her.

She also looks different. She's wearing a simple white cotton jumper, white cotton anklets, and a pair of flat white patent-leather shoes with straps. She's even wound a girlish white ribbon through her curly hair, like an especially virginal sixteen-year-old. She looks as unlike her usual leather-and-leopard-skin self as possible. It's disconcerting. But she doesn't comment on it, and neither do I. I'm much too eager to get to my journal entry. "This time," I tell her proudly, "I didn't write it on paper towels. I bought this." I fumble inside my embroidered drawstring pocketbook for the cream-colored notebook I stopped off and bought on my way home yesterday from TAG.

"Okay, so read." Her voice still sounds distracted. "But just so you know," she goes on, "I quit smoking yesterday, and I'm feeling very edgy."

So that explains what else seems so different about her today. No cigarettes. No smoke. I notice for the first time that the ashtray is clean. "Congratulations," I say automatically. It's what I say to anyone who's quit any addictive habit: cigarettes, coffee, drinking, drugs, late-night radio call-in shows, whatever. But really, I'm feeling more stunned than congratulatory. It's impossible for me to imagine Shara-Rose, session after session, week after week, not smoking. Almost as impossible as imagining her looking like a sixteen-year-old virgin. But both seem to be happening before my disbelieving eyes. Once, on some low-budget cable TV talk show, I saw a bearded psychologist who'd written a book about how patients have trouble accepting change on their therapists' parts. "When I lose or gain even five pounds," he'd said to the host, stroking his pointy beard, "my most insecure patients have been known to break down and weep." At the time, I'd thought he was either exaggerating or crazy, but now I'm not so sure. Because the truth is that the idea of a Shara-Rose not addicted to nicotine unnerves the hell out of me. I wonder whether her white outfit is supposed to symbolize her new smoke-free life.

But rather than spending my time and money thinking about her cigarette habit, I'd much rather read my journal entry to her. "I'm proud of this entry," I say. "It's philosophical." She doesn't say a word. For the first time I notice something else that's different about her today. She's no longer sitting still; now she's vigorously chewing gum and gnawing on her thumbnails. Two new habits to replace the old.

I open the cream-colored notebook and read.

Dear Beatle George, You're undoubtedly an excellent person with whom to discuss "Forgiveness: Pro and Con." Because, from what I've heard, there were lots of arguments, temper tantrums, and betrayals among the Beatles, before and after your break-up. My immediate concern, of course—philosophical matters aside—is what to do about my own George. Shall I just call him up tomorrow and say, "I forgive you"? After all, to err is human, and to forgive, divine. And I'm no saint myself. But, then again, what George did—or is still doing, perhaps?—with Nicole Burden can hardly be called an "error," can it? And is divinity necessarily worth aspiring to?

Yet just about everyone I know expects me to be able to forgive and forget. Just like that. Which brings me, inevitably, back to the baby issue: shouldn't two people be at peace within themselves and within their relationship before they have a child? I'd love to hear what you, the Spiritual Beatle, have to say about this.

Well, I sign off now.... Ever your fan, Babette.

I look up. Shara-Rose is sitting on her hands now. Her eyes are closed. Her brow is wrinkled. She's still chewing gum. She doesn't say anything. I have a feeling that she's been sitting there, throughout my reading, thinking exclusively about cigarettes. "Shara-Rose," I ask indignantly, "did you hear a single word?"

She opens her eyes. "Of course I did." But her expression is completely distracted. "Your prose is turning slightly purple, but despite that, I can tell that it was written from the heart. I also can tell that you're still suffering. And why shouldn't you be? It may be fashionable to take adultery lightly these days. But you trusted George. Period. And trust has nothing to do with fashion. _Trust_ is your issue, not sex. That's why you didn't sleep with Trent or Carlos, you know, or any of those other men you've been fantasizing about, including the cute cabdriver and the loinclothed actors in *Early Man*, and even Ricky, that old high-school weasel. The sex part always came easily for you, no pun intended. It's the trust part you have problems with. I keep telling you, Babette, you idealize George—which is really a very narcissistic thing to do, by the way, and don't take that as a criticism, because lots of us do it— idealize our loved ones. It's, like, a way of idealizing *ourselves*. I mean, very deep down, in your deepest unconscious, irrational id, some little stubborn part of you really thinks you've landed yourself a Beatle! You think you're Patti Boyd!"

I start to frown, but before I can say a word, she goes on.

"I'm being very blunt here, Babette, I know, but please don't get flip with me. Listen to me. Trust me: One of the reasons you *won't* speak to George is because you *can't* speak to him. You're terrified to. Because then you'll have to see that he's just a real guy, a guy from a farm, a guy who chose a career in the *very* cutthroat, very lucrative, frequently lacking-in-integrity world of corporate law—quite the opposite of a wife who's dedicated herself, heart and soul, to the world of cutting-edge, total-integrity, avant-garde theater. And, on top of that, to coin a street phrase, he made a big mistake recently: He thought with his dick, not his brains, pardon my French, again. However, now back to shrink lingo, you're going to have to confront what we call a 'crack in the narcissistic projection,' because you *have* to talk to him about what's happened. This is quite common, by the way. Lots of marriages go through some *very* difficult and fundamental changes over this stuff. Usually, though, there's a little bit more *dialogue* between the partners during the process. But the main thing is—he ain't no Beatle, Babette."

Despite the fact that I'm feeling more and more hurt—and frightened, and even a bit ashamed of myself for being such a perpetual _groupie_—I know, too, for the first time that there is real truth to her words. So I force myself to sit quietly, with the leather sticking to my thighs, without interrupting her with some reflexive flip remark.

"Anyway," she goes on, "I honestly believe that you're a lot closer to finding peace about George than you think you are. You're a lot closer to finding peace about him than I am about not smoking."

I ignore her references to herself. "So are you saying that I'm going to go back to George? Or that I'm not?"

"That's entirely up to you. I never tell you what to do."

I can't believe she always says this to me—that she never tells me what to do—with a straight face, considering that she's frequently the bossiest shrink in the universe. But since my time in her office is also my money, once again it doesn't seem worth it to point out the irony of her own words to her. Besides, she's obviously still thinking mostly about cigarettes, I can tell; she's still sitting on her hands, and I wonder if she has any circulation left. She blows an impressively large bubble with her chewing gum.

"And what about this Dr. First?" I decide to forge ahead with the practical things on my mind. "Do you really think I should go to see him with George?"

Her bubble pops. "First, you decide about First." In her typically mercurial style, she's now laughing uproariously at her own little excuse of a joke. She resumes her vigorous gum chewing. "But listen," she leans forward, no longer laughing, now very intense looking, "there's something I'd like to discuss with you. And what I want to discuss with you isn't easy. But it's got to be said." She takes a deep breath. "Damn, I could kill someone for a smoke."

Warily, I lean back on the sticky leather sofa.

"Don't worry," she says, "there's no point in my killing you. You don't carry cigarettes." She sighs. "I'm beginning the process of ending my practice."

Since all I had for breakfast this morning was a bowl of chocolate chocolate chip ice cream and a glass of orange juice, I know that I can't be drunk. Which means that she's just said what I think she's just said. It doesn't seem fair: If, toward some therapeutic end, she wants to upset me, she could simply have announced that the sky is falling. That would have been kinder. And easier to believe. Therapists don't stop practicing in New York City. They can't afford to.

"It'll be a gradual process, of course," she says. "You and I will meet a few more times. More, if you need to. And we'll discuss what ending the therapeutic relationship means to both of us. I'll answer whatever questions you may have, and I'll recommend other therapists, if you want me to. Believe me, I don't expect my patients to have to go cold turkey the way I'm having to with cigarettes."

Stopping smoking is nothing compared to this. This is a bombshell. An earthquake. A tidal wave. A nuclear war. Every natural and unnatural disaster I can think of. "Why?" I'm nearly shouting. "Why are you doing this?"

She answers in a very modulated, subdued tone. "The reason is…I want to make it as a singer. I mean, *really* make it. To take the next step." She leans forward, growing slightly more animated again. "Since you're in such a philosophical mood yourself today, let's call it the existential leap of faith. I want to go after a record contract. I want to make videos. I'd like to try my hand at producing. And I want to stop performing at dumps like Tarts. But in order for these things to happen, music has got to be my full-time career. At least for a while. If it doesn't work out, or if I change my mind, I can always resume my practice. But I'll never know if I can do it unless I try. The bottom line is this: I've changed. The music part of my life is becoming my whole life. It's simple, I guess. Scary, too."

I'd always thought that *she*—unlike me—was so content. That, in her wacky way, she was doing exactly what she felt destined to do. "But what about us?" I ask. "Your needy and dependent patients? All of us anxiety-ridden types who have been terrified since birth of being abandoned? You're abandoning us all. Worst of all, you're abandoning _me!_ I'm not cured yet." "You don't need a cure. You're not ill. Confused sometimes, but who isn't? You've been asking yourself some hard questions. Should you forgive a husband who's deliberately deceived you for quite a while, or shouldn't you? Should you—pardon that dreadful shrink lingo again—risk a 'crack in your narcissistic projection,' by speaking to him again, or shouldn't you? Should you, after years of monogamy, have an affair with another man, a very attractive, intelligent, avant-garde playwright who's been sleeping in the bedroom next door to yours at night, and ogling your legs in those provocative shorts during the day, until you're both driving each other rather mad with lust—or shouldn't you? Should you continue to devote your work life to TAG, or should you begin to devote yourself to _Hard-Boiled?_ Should you have a baby, or shouldn't you? What's so sick about asking questions like that? It's the people who never ask questions in the first place who aren't healthy."

I refuse to be heartened by her upbeat diagnosis. "Is that why you're dressed all in white?" I ask bitterly. "Going out into the music world a virgin?"

She smiles and pops another bubble. "No. My mother is coming in from Florida this afternoon for a visit, and it makes her so happy when I dress like this. It seems like such a little thing to do to make her happy. Because, unfortunately, she's going to be very, very unhappy when she hears about my decision to give up practicing therapy."

"I'll never forgive you," is what I think I'm about to say, "for taking me so far and then abandoning me like this, during my time of crisis." But that's not what I say. "I wish you the best of luck," is what I hear myself saying, instead. "And I forgive you."

"Thank you, Babette," she says seriously, "I appreciate the sentiment. But you know, I'm not doing anything that requires forgiving."

24

After the session, reeling from Shara-Rose's announcement, I walk slowly home, down Broadway. For some reason, all of the panhandlers I encounter this morning seem threatening and hostile. Not that I can entirely blame them. I must appear to be their enemy: well fed, good clothes on my back, a roof over my head. But when a man wearing a sweater tied around his head and newspapers wrapped all over his feet, lunges at me, I feel frightened. And angry. And I wonder how small children must feel when they witness such things happening on their streets. And how the mothers of the children must feel. Finally, one panhandler tells me to have a nice day; gratefully, I give him a dollar. "Bless you, Veronica," he says to me, which I assume refers to my Veronica Lake hairdo. I give him another dollar. Meanwhile, I'm also trying to envision my life without Shara-Rose. As I've often said, when I defended her to Maya, "She's odd, true, but she's smart, intuitive, and warm, and what else matters in a shrink?"

As usual, the first thing I do when I get back to Lydia's is to pet

Flaca, who's come to the door to greet me, and the second thing is to check the answering machine for messages. The only message is from Carlos, whose grant money is all gone, and who's out on his shift driving a taxi. He and I work together on _Hard-Boiled_ only late at night now, when he's exhausted from driving all day long, although he's never too exhausted to stare desirously at my legs. "Don't worry," he keeps telling me, "I'm used to working like this, in the nooks and crannies of life." But his message this morning sounds completely rushed and frazzled. Against a background of car horns, blaring radios, and construction site drilling, he shouts, "Remember! Lunch! Armstrong's!"

But despite Shara-Rose's news, I haven't forgotten: He and I have arranged a noon lunch date at Armstrong's with two of the members of the Microtonal Music Collective.

I rewind the tape and erase Carlos's message. I'm surprised that there's no kvetchy message from Jay. And no message from George. Usually, by this time, George has left his daily message for me.

Before I leave the kitchen, I make a slight adjustment to the Barbie Doll's backhand, and then I head into the bedroom to change my clothes and get ready for lunch. Flaca, who's followed me, watches with what I interpret as an approving look as I slip out of the tank top and shorts and into a trim-fitting, above-the-knee-length short khaki dress, which still shows off my legs, but is a bit more businesslike for this meeting with the Microtonals. It occurs to me that with my forties movie-star hairdo, I'm ready to appear in a World War II movie as a sexy, but patriotic, WAC.

When I get to Armstrong's, Carlos, wearing his mirrored sunglasses and his dungaree jacket, is already there, seated at a table in the back, drinking a large mug of coffee.

He looks so attractive, I wonder again whether I made the right decision about not sleeping with him. As soon as I'm seated, though, I put aside that thought and I tell him about Shara-Rose's bombshell.

"I think it's great."

Although I can't see his eyes through his mirrored sunglasses, his voice sounds sincere enough. "How can you say that?" I protest. "It's like a world-famous brain surgeon deciding in mid-life to become an acrobat."

"It is?" He takes a large swallow of coffee, and wipes his brow.

"Yes. It is. Just to indulge some adolescent whim, this highly skilled brain surgeon is abandoning hundreds of people whose lives she could save."

"You're hardly in danger of losing your life," he says.

I frown. "It was just an analogy."

"Well, I've got a better analogy. How about this: Shara-Rose's decision to become a rock singer is like Babette Bliss's decision to take a risk and actually write a play, herself, rather than just sitting around her office all day on her behind and deciding what gets performed and what doesn't."

"That's a lousy analogy." My voice is huffy. Carlos is starting to irritate me, and he suddenly looks a lot less attractive. For the first time, the way he slurps his coffee gets on my nerves. "First of all," I tell him, still huffily, "my job at TAG is a lot more than my sitting around all day long and passing judgment on struggling artists. Second of all, nobody is being abandoned by my decision to write a play. So it's not analogous at all."

"Jay thinks you're abandoning him. And George thinks you're abandoning him. That's at least two." He slurps his coffee even more loudly than before.

"But they're both being ridiculous and you know it." Carlos has never gotten on my nerves quite this much before. "I'm on vacation from TAG. Period. Arts administrators are real people too, you know. And real people—especially hard-working, exhausted, underpaid real people—deserve vacations. And George is the one who had the affair, so I'd say he's the one who abandoned me."

"All I'm saying, Babette," Carlos says politely, "is that your situation and Shara-Rose's situation are not without their similarities."

The waitress comes over. Carlos asks for a refill of coffee. I order a seltzer.

After she's gone, he continues. "I think that Shara-Rose is being courageous. And I think that you are, too."

I frown again, but I feel less irritated with him now. It's difficult to remain irritated with someone who's calling me courageous. It doesn't happen every day. The last time was when I was a little girl. My mother and I had been strolling in Bronx Park, when a big, ferocious-looking dog started to bark wildly at me. I didn't flinch. "That was very courageous of you," my mother said, pulling me away from the dog, not realizing that I'd been too traumatized to move a muscle or make a sound, but that inwardly, I had already died a thousand deaths in the dog's meaty paws.

But before I get so caught up reliving that moment that I develop a permanent dog phobia, I spot a woman standing in the doorway. She's an aging flower child: Her long, thick, graying hair flows loose, with a crooked part down the middle. She's wearing rimless, octagonal-shaped eyeglasses, and a flowered Indian dress with flowing, butterfly-shaped sleeves.

"Look," I whisper to Carlos, "a Microtonal."

Nodding, Carlos rises and strides to the doorway. A moment later, he brings her back to the table.

I'm enthralled by her looks. She appears so sure of her identity, so resolute about her place in history. Maya loves to poke fun at aging hippies. "They're stuck, Babette," she says, "absolutely stuck, like Crazy Glue, to a decade that's kaput." But I love to imagine their steadfast lives, and to wonder what would have happened if George and I had chosen that life together. If we lived on a commune, wearing tie-dyed clothes and eating only vegetables from our own garden. If we had babies named Sunshine and Rainbow. Would things have been very, very different? Or, eventually, would

I still have wanted to do more with my life than I was doing? And would he have had an affair with one of the hippie ladies on the commune, perhaps a raven-haired seductress named Moon Flower?

As is my habit these days with everyone I meet, the instant the Microtonal sits down across from me, I want to know everything about her. Whether she's married, whether she sleeps around or is faithful, whether she has children, and whether marriage, mother-hood, and microtonal music make her happy. "Babette Bliss," Carlos introduces us, "Susan Bernstein."

"Bernstein it is," she says in a warm voice, "and musical I may be, but I'm not Leonard's rebellious daughter. I'm no relation."

We shake hands. I like her already.

Carlos is checking his watch. He's on a cabbie's lunch hour. For every minute he sits here, he's missing a fare.

"Paul will be here soon," she explains to Carlos. "He often runs a bit late." She turns to me. "The collective is extremely excited about *Hard-Boiled*. The last full-fledged gig we had was about a year ago. We played an opening at a Hoboken art gallery." She runs a hand through her thick gray hair. "Between gigs, I'm a social worker."

She's wearing a ring on her wedding finger, but it's not a tradi-tional wedding ring. It's a silver puzzle ring. It would be much too pushy for me to come right out and ask her about her marital, sex-ual, and maternal statuses. So I wish that Carlos, who's always less worried about what other people think of him than I am, would ask her instead. But he wouldn't even think of it; he's handling his grief over Martha differently than I'm handling mine over George. He's not looking for answers in the life of every person he meets.

"There's Paul," Susan announces, pointing to the doorway.

I turn to look, expecting to see an aging male hippie with a long gray ponytail and a scraggly beard. But the man standing in the doorway looks like a well-fed, baby-faced fraternity boy, twenty-two, at most. His dark brown hair is neatly combed, and he's wearing a white shirt, chinos, and leather moccasins.

Susan waves at him, and he comes over and joins us. She does the introductions. "Babette Bliss and Carlos Carlos, this is Paul McArthur."

Paul grins: a boyish, eager-to-please grin.

I shake his hand. The waitress comes over. She's wearing a white tank top, and as she bends over to write down our orders, I spot Paul staring down her top and looking boyishly excited by the free show.

I order the marinated mussels. Carlos orders the Haitian cod and yet another refill of coffee. Paul orders a cheeseburger with french fries and a Coke, which seems appropriately adolescent. Susan orders a salad and a glass of water, which also seems appropriate; she's undoubtedly a vegetarian.

The waitress departs. Susan turns to Paul. "I was just telling Babette and Carlos about the collective."

"Right," he says. "Being a microtonal musician is a bit like being a member of the Flat Earth Society."

I'm impressed with Paul. Fraternity boys usually don't make references to the Flat Earth Society.

"Now, there's an idea," Carlos says excitedly, making a note on an index card he pulls out of the pocket of his denim jacket. "The Flat Earth Society! What a study in alienation.... I can really see possibilities there. Can't you, Babette?" He looks meaningfully at me, and I have a feeling he's going to ask me to work on another piece. But I'm still so insecure about my contributions to *Hard-Boiled*, I can't begin to imagine ever tackling another project.

"So, Paul," I ask, ignoring Carlos's meaningful look, "what do you do besides microtonaling?"

"I play violin with a chamber music group. And I tutor kids in math."

"I'm curious," I continue, as I try to remove a stubborn mussel from its shell, "how many members does the collective have?"

"There's Tadashi," Paul says, chewing on his plastic straw like a kid, "who's in Japan right now, visiting his family. He owns a computer business. And Edna, who sings in supper clubs, and Dino, who plays sax around town with jazz groups."

"And Jenny, who's a Buddhist and drives a taxi," Susan adds. "She also designs a lot of the instruments we use."

Carlos grimaces at the word *taxi*.

"It's so wonderful," Susan says, excitedly waving a slice of cucumber around with her fork, "that you both appreciate microtonal music so much."

"It really is cool," Paul says.

I decide not to mention that I'd never even heard of microtonal music until very, very recently, and that I'm not yet sure that I do appreciate it. I concentrate on my mussels.

"I read hard-boiled novels myself," Paul says. "Only between gigs, of course." He grins boyishly again.

"So does Adam," Susan says. "It makes me furious." She explains. "Adam is my son. He's a sophomore at Rutgers. I encourage him to read the classics. Tolstoi. Chekhov. But no. He's only interested in the trashiest, most lurid paperback novels." She sounds genuinely puzzled.

"Do you have other children?" I ask.

"Two others. Karen, who's studying dance, and Billy, who's still in high school." She sounds much happier discussing these two. I'm a little in awe of her: Raising three children can't be a picnic.

Before I can ask Susan about her marital status, Paul clears his throat and says, brightly, "And I'm a brand-new father."

I'm shocked: How can this baby-faced kid who likes to look down waitresses' shirts already have his own kid?

"My wife gave birth three weeks ago," he says, proudly. He reaches into his wallet and takes out a photo of a red-faced, squalling infant, whose sex I can't determine. Carlos and I make appropriate sounds of pleasure. Then Carlos looks at his watch again.

I feel jealous of this kid with his own kid. Has he, at his age, already achieved the inner peace, sense of purpose, and self-knowledge necessary to be a wonderful, nurturing father? I doubt it.

The waitress returns and removes our plates. And Paul, the new daddy, stares down her top again with completely unabashed, adolescent glee.

"Babette," Carlos says, "why don't you read a small portion from _Hard-Boiled_, to give Susan and Paul a feel for it?"

My hands are shaking as I pull my _Hard-Boiled_ notebook—just a spiral notebook, not nearly as nice as my cream-colored journal —from the embroidered pocketbook. Susan and Paul are looking at me expectantly.

"It's very rough," I apologize. "It's just a draft. A very, very, very rough first draft."

Carlos gives me an encouraging look. Trying to will my anxiety away, I take a deep breath. I begin to read, in as clear and strong a voice as I can muster:

The curtain rises. We see a spotlessly clean locker room, filled with impossibly green plastic plants. Shining, full-length mirrors are hanging on all the walls. Phillipa Marlowe enters from stage right. She's tall and lean, wearing a trench coat and a hat pulled low over her face. She sits on the bench, straddling it aggressively. Eerie microtonal music begins to play offstage.

Philippa addresses the audience. Her voice is tough and sexy. "Three rich dames have turned up murdered right here, on this bench, in the last three weeks. And me," she says, "I'm supposed to find out who's been knocking off the Misses Liposuction and why."

She stands. She unbuttons her raincoat. Underneath she's wearing a pair of jogging shorts and a jogger's mesh tank top. "The thing is, I ain't got the time for this case. I'm working on a TV pilot. I wanna make some bucks. Being a gumshoe is gonna keep me in the gutter for the rest of my life. And I'm sick of it." She bends down to tie the shoelaces of *her aerobics shoes. "Oh well," she says, "time for class." She exits stage right. Offstage, we hear the voice of an aerobics instructor, "Now ladies, move those hips, that's right, one and two…" Her instructions are out of tune, along with the microtonal music.*

"Well," I say breathlessly, "that gives you an idea." I feel shy. And mortified.

But Susan's eyes are starry. "We could do it. Absolutely."

"It's cool," Paul says.

"Great." Carlos signals the waitress for the check. "This is on me."

"On us," I insist.

Susan and Paul thank us. Carlos and I split the bill, and we all rise. "You read beautifully, Babette," Susan says. Embarrassed, I thank her. "Oh, one other thing," I say, shyly. I tell them about TAG and Acme Developers. "There's going to be a demonstration. Maybe the Microtonal Music Collective could come and lend their support." I'm surprised that I'm doing this. Maybe I *am* working for TAG again, after all. My vacation appears to have just ended.

"We'll be there," Susan assures me. She and Paul wave good-bye and then head west to liberate their cars from a parking lot on Eleventh Avenue.

"This is going to work out, I can tell," Carlos says happily to me.

I nod. I like him again. And really, he wasn't slurping his coffee all that loudly. "But Carlos," I ask, "don't you think that Paul is sort of young to be a father?"

"I didn't think about it." He shrugs. "Listen, I'll give you a ride back to Lydia's."

Although Lydia's apartment is only two blocks away, I figure, why not. He can't be a worse driver than any other New York cabbie.

"So, Carlos," I say, settling into the back seat of his cab, which is parked on Tenth, "what have you decided to do about Martha?"

"I've decided," he says, pulling out into the street fast, without looking, "to try to forget Martha." He abruptly cuts off another cab, and I hold my breath. "To get on with my life. To write plays, drive a cab, see my friends, and meet other women. I miss sex." On the word *sex*, he turns around to face me, and I grip the door handle in terror, as we narrowly avoid hitting a bicyclist. "You had your chance, Babette," he says flirtatiously.

I smile wanly, and I'm pleased when he turns around again and starts looking at the road.

"Any time you change your mind, just let me know." He looks at me in his rearview mirror.

"Carlos, I'm flattered." I miss sex too, I think, but I stop myself from saying it aloud.

"You're not *just* flattered," he says, honking his horn at the same time as the cab he had cut off now cuts him off. "Those kisses we exchanged were the real thing. You're also attracted to me. Very attracted. I know you are."

"Okay, Carlos, I *am*. Very attracted. But now that we're artistic collaborators, it's just impossible."

He turns around and smiles at me. I see my face reflected in his mirrored sunglasses. A bus driver begins to honk at him. He turns back to face the road. "I disagree," he says. "Collaborators make the best lovers. They're in sync in unique ways. Once, when I was still in college, I collaborated on a multimedia piece called *Love/ Danger* with a girl in my dorm, and we used to do the most amazing things to each other, night after night, things drawn right from the pages of the script itself."

I feel immediately jealous of this girl, and I try not to picture what "amazing" things they were doing to each other. "Well, I wouldn't know, Carlos." I keep my voice and manner astonishingly calm, although I'm unable to resist a mental picture of Carlos intricately tying a blond coed to a bedpost with colorful silk scarves. "You are, after all, my first collaborator. But the thing is— as long as George and I are still married, even if we're separated, and even if he's had an affair, well, I've got this crazy bug about *my* not complicating things further...." I'm glad that Carlos and I are having this talk, and that we're being honest with each other, even if it means that now I'm more certain than ever that he's exactly the kind of lover that could keep a hot-blooded, uninhibited, aggressive Jewish girl from the Bronx happy in bed, and even if it also means that he keeps turning around to stare at me instead of keeping his eyes on the road.

With a horrendous screech, he pulls his cab up to the curb outside Lydia's. "I know," he says. "You just can't be with another man right now. Or just not yet. Maybe deep down you're a very old-fashioned avant-gardist. Or maybe you've just got too much ego and pride invested in being the faithful one in your marriage, after your wild past, which, by the way, I've heard plenty of rumors about. I sure wish I'd known you back then."

I feel myself blushing. I sort of wish the same thing, although that's not the point, and I know better than to say so to Carlos.

"Still," he goes on, "if I can't have you, then I think that you and George should try to work things out together. I've been thinking that maybe Maya, Shara-Rose, and George are right that you're a little bit crazy or something, still refusing to speak to him. That's what I think."

"So you're another one." Now I'm annoyed at him again. I exit from his cab without saying good-bye. I watch as he pulls out into traffic with another loud screech. I head into the building, and ride up the elevator, feeling more confused than ever by Carlos's words.

Stepping out of the elevator, I see George, leaning against the door of Lydia's apartment.

25

I stand stock-still in front of the elevator. George and I stare at each other. His expression strikes me as inscrutable, and I feel equally inscrutable to myself. I'm cut off and distanced from my own response to seeing him standing there, in his crisp-looking light tan suit, waiting for me, as though he knew that I'd be returning to Lydia's at exactly this moment.

I can't feel what expression is on my face: It could be an involuntary nervous smile, or it could be a frown. Or I could be blushing hotly, or turning pale. Maybe I have no feelings about seeing George. Maybe I've become numb. On the other hand, maybe it's because I have so many contradictory feelings that I can't feel any one more than another. In either case, the end result is the same: I'm standing here as though in a trance.

He clears his throat. I look away, and for the first time I notice the green-and-white flowered wallpaper in the hallway. I hear the elevator creak as it moves to another floor. I hear a vacuum cleaner whirring inside someone's apartment. I also hear the sound of someone, down the hall and out of my sight, opening and closing an apartment door. A lock turning. A second lock. The jangling of keys. A dog's whiny little bark. Footsteps.

Finally the person comes into view. A heavily made-up woman wearing a white velour jogging suit. She's walking one of those hideously cropped poodles on a leash. It occurs to me, even in my daze, that she looks like one of the Misses Liposuction from *Hard-Boiled*. With annoyance, she looks first at me, then at George. But George, still leaning against Lydia's door, doesn't even glance at her. Reaching over me, she rings for the elevator. Her poodle starts barking and snapping viciously at my ankles. This rouses me into action. Although, when I start walking towards the apartment, I don't feel as though I'm doing it entirely of my own volition. I still have that uneasy trancelike feeling, as though someone else, some invisible friend or enemy, is guiding me.

This feeling of being guided by someone else stays with me as I reach into the pocket of my khaki dress and pull out the key to the apartment. This invisible guide steadies my hand so that it doesn't tremble as I turn the key in the lock and open the door. But as soon as the door is open, that mysterious invisible someone else seems to vanish, and I'm faced with a choice. I can either slam the door in George's face, or I can let him in. He's waiting, not moving, staring at me intensely, clearly letting me choose. I hold the door open, and he follows me inside. He shuts the door. We stand, facing each other. Flaca, who's probably been awakened from a nap, is nuzzling at my legs.

Squaring my shoulders, I take a deep breath, feeling like a soldier about to enter battle. Babette's Silent Period has come to its end. There's bound to be yelling and screaming. I'll accuse him of things. He'll accuse me back. Perhaps one of us will become violent: a push, a shove, a slap. Violence between us is something I once would never have believed possible. But once I never would have believed that quiet, sensible George would be the one having an affair, either. Or that I would leave him. So anything is possible.

As though sensing something big in the air that would be best to avoid, Flaca heads into the kitchen. George takes me into his arms and begins to kiss me. I expect my body to stiffen, to resist. But it doesn't. I'm not stiff, I'm not resisting even slightly. I'm pliant, vulnerable, and aroused.

He places his hand on the small of my back, and I shudder. And it's me who's stepping back, taking his hand, leading him into the small bedroom, closing the bedroom door. There's no invisible someone guiding me now. It's me, definitely me, all by myself, willingly, independently, closing the bedroom door, lying down on the bed, shutting my eyes and delighting in feeling the pressure of George's body as he gets on top of me, feeling his lips against my own yielding lips, and his smooth, newly shaved, fragrant skin rubbing aginst my own skin.

It's me who begins to unbutton his shirt, who places my hand on his bare chest, and who obediently raises my arms over my head so that he can pull my dress off, which he does with both care and urgency.

We still haven't spoken a single word to each other. And yet we're making love. It's a lovemaking that is, I know, born from desire, tenderness, frustration, and rage. And from other things, as well. Things I can't name or understand now, in the throes of this unexpected passion.

We make love for a long time, our eyes closed, our bodies moving violently, both of us sweating, both of us breathing hard.

When we stop, still we don't speak. Silently, we lie next to each other, our bodies not touching. Not fully believing that this has happened, I touch my own wet skin, as though for verification of the heat of the moment. Then I lie still again, waiting for my heart to stop pounding.

Even though it's midday, the room is dark. For the first time since I've moved into Lydia's apartment, I wish I'd taken the bright, airy bedroom so that sunlight would pour in through the window. The one window in this bedroom faces an airshaft.

George begins to stroke my hip, softly at first, and then harder. Soon we're making love again. But still without speaking a word to each other. Still with our eyes closed.

Again, when it's over, we lie next to each other. I'm even hotter and sweatier than before.

At last, George speaks, breaking the silence between us. "Babette," he says, in a sweet and wondering tone. That's all he says. He sounds so ingenuous, like a child discovering and acknowledging my existence for the first time. A child who hopes, by naming me aloud, to comprehend me. And to possess me. To make me part of his personal universe.

I look at him. I look into his eyes, and I want to say it: *I forgive you.* Like an overzealous coach, I urge myself, the reluctant athlete, to go ahead and say it.

But I can't. Despite lovemaking. Despite the innocence in his voice. Despite the way my body feels: loved and desired and nurtured all at once. Because, despite all these things, my body feels something else, too. It feels bruised, like a tender fruit that's been roughed up a bit too much in some places, with the marks to prove it.

I can't say it. So I do the best I can. "I'd like you to go now," I say softly to him, and I pause and take a deep breath, "but I will go to see Dr. First with you."

I close my eyes. And I don't open them again for what feels like years. Not until I'm sure that George has risen from the bed, has gotten dressed, and has gone out the door.

26

It's been two days since George's unexpected visit. Our appointment with Dr. First is scheduled for today at three o'clock. The building is prewar and elegant, on Central Park West, with three snooty-looking doormen and three mirrored, gold-trimmed elevators. Arbitrarily, I choose the center elevator. As I ride upstairs to Dr. First's office on the seventeenth floor, I'm horrified to hear a piped-in, saccharine muzak version of The Beatles' "Why Don't We Do It in the Road."

Already I'm not in the greatest mood as I open the door to Dr. First's waiting room. My initial, overwhelming impression is that I'm drowning in a sea of beige: beige walls, beige rug, beige armchairs. Even the photographs hanging on the beige walls are of beige-colored, generic-looking beaches.

George is sitting in one of the beige chairs. I'm grateful that he's not wearing a single item of beige clothing. He's dressed casually, in neatly pressed blue jeans, a black polo shirt, and polished white sneakers, which means that he's taken the day off from work. Which means he's really serious about this couple therapy business. He looks up at me. There's nothing inscrutable about his expression now. He looks as awkward and uncomfortable as I feel. After all, only a few days ago, estranged and silent though we may be, we were making passionate love on Lydia's bed.

But before we have even one moment alone together in which to become accustomed to each other's presence here in this un-known shrink's waiting room, the unknown shrink's office door opens, and a man, presumably the unknown shrink himself, walks briskly toward us, his hand outstretched.

"Good afternoon. I'm Dr. First." He speaks in carefully modu-lated tones which fit right in with the beige decor. "Please come inside."

Like two embarrassed schoolchildren being called into the principal's office, George and I shuffle inside, heads down, not looking at each other.

Dr. First closes his office door. "Make yourselves comfortable," he says, as he sits down behind a large beige desk, on a plush beige chair that looks as though it cost him a small fortune.

George, like me, is hanging back hesitantly, looking around the office. The office, too, is a beige-lover's delight. Another beige rug. And more beige photographs of beige beaches hanging on beige walls. I wish that Maya would barge in, uninvited, and plunk down a few hot pink vases, candelabras, and end tables.

There's also a beige sofa along one wall. But I can tell that Dr. First intends for us to sit in the two beige armchairs in the center of the room, which, I suspect, are where the angry husbands and wives coming for couple therapy sit and duke it out.

Sighing, I sit in one of the chairs, leaning forward and crossing my legs in the aggressive way the tough boys back in high school used to.

George sits in the other chair.

I give Dr. First the once-over. He's as bland as his decor. Naturally, he's wearing a beige V-neck sweater. He's not at all the kind of person I would have expected Shara-Rose to recommend, or even to know. I expected a male version of Shara-Rose herself: leather pants, an earring, photographs of rock singers on the walls. I'm insulted that Shara-Rose has sent us to see this guy. Maybe she sent us to this nerd because, deep down, she doesn't really want us to get back together.

"Fine," Dr. First says, approving our seating choices. "Why don't both of you explain what brings you here?" His voice is so modulated he sounds half-asleep.

George nods. "I was hoping," he says seriously, looking at Dr. First, "to explain to Babette...," he turns to face me, "...how I allowed what happened...to happen." He doesn't add anything else, and both he and Dr. First look expectantly at me.

Shifting uneasily in the beige armchair, I uncross and recross my legs, still maintaining my tough boy's attitude. I don't like Dr. First's office. And I don't like Dr. First. "I'll hear George out," I can hear the resistance in my own voice, "but I have nothing to say at this point." I feel nervous, although I try not to show it; after all, I've just retreated another few steps during battle.

"Fine," the ever-polite Dr. First says. "George, feel free to begin."

George doesn't miss a beat. "I didn't realize it, Babette," he says, staring intensely at me as he speaks. "If I had realized it, I would have told you. It happened without my knowing it."

I'm riveted by the intensity of his gaze. And even though I've just gone on record that I'm not going to say a word, I'm already itching to interrupt, to ask what the hell _it_ refers to. Is _it_ a euphemism for—as Maya's ex-hubby, Merv, used to say—_porking_ another woman? But that can't be it, because there's no way he could have been porking Nicole without _knowing_ that he was doing _it_. Well, no matter what _it_ is, I refuse to ask. If he's going to be vague, that's his business. After all, I'm still not convinced that anything he can say will make a difference.

"I mean, I'd grown bored and frustrated with my job, and yet my job had, unfortunately, become too much of my life. And I was feeling trapped and pressured. And angry at myself for having allowed it to happen to me. I'd decided that I would never become one of those arrogant lawyers in the pinstriped suits. But instead I became something else, someone so cut off from myself, so haughty about my self-control, that I might have been better off becoming one of those aggressive loudmouth types."

I look over at Dr. First, who's looking down at his desk. I wonder if he's even listening. He doesn't stir, and I look back at George, whose eyes are still fixed on me.

"I wanted something more out of life, but I not only didn't know what I wanted, I was so detached that I didn't even know that I *wanted* anything. It's so easy for me, I've come to see, to lead the unexamined life, to go through every day by rote, without passion.... But I didn't see that in myself. And neither did you."

I still stick to my end of the bargain; I refuse to say a word, even though I feel that he's accusing me, in a way, of failing him for not recognizing his unhappiness, for not seeing that he, too, had his own sets of crises. *Not fair*, I want to cry out, but I clench my teeth instead.

"And then I got angry at you, Babette. For not saving me. But I was so cut off, I didn't even realize that I was angry. And I was jealous too, jealous because I knew you'd had such an uninhibited past, while I'd been a sheltered small-town boy, and then a sheltered, hardworking law student, and then your basic workaholic lawyer. I never had time to sow my oats."

Again, I want to protest: How can these things he's saying be true? I loved this man. I would have noticed. But then again, he wasn't really spending his time with me, was he? He'd been spending nearly all of his time at the office. He'd been avoiding me for quite a while—consciously or unconsciously, I realize now—probably even before he and Nicole began their affair. Perhaps, in the end, it's really *this* that has hurt and enraged me even more than the fact of his affair: that he hadn't turned to *me*, that he hadn't appeared to need *me*. He turned to a spoiled rich bitch—an Ice Queen—instead of to *me*. So does all this mean that I really have mythified him and idealized him, as Shara-Rose keeps saying? Have I completely romanticized our marriage, even gone so far as to have imagined our love because of my desperate need to trust *someone*, and because of my fervent desire to prove that I—lusty, never-before-faithful Babette—could have an all-American, apple-pie marriage, with no fooling around?

"So I looked elsewhere," he says, "to Nicole."

I'm determined, despite all my inner turmoil, to show no response to her name.

"And Nicole was looking for someone, too. For someone to rescue her. Nicole is…" and here, for the first time, he hesitates.

What is he afraid of saying to me at this point? All sorts of phrases come to my mind: *Nicole is…the apple of my eye, the light of my life, more of a woman than you'll ever be…*Tensely, I wait.

"Nicole has a drug habit," he says.

I laugh out loud in disbelief. He can't, he just can't, expect me to believe that the cool-as-a-cucumber Mayflower Miss is a cokehead.

"Really," he says, sounding annoyed that I don't believe him.

I shrug to let him know that one way or another—cokehead or not—she isn't *my* problem.

He's trying not to sound annoyed now; I can see him deliberately rearranging his features—a lawyer's trick. He goes on, in a much calmer tone. "Anyway, that's how she and I first grew… close. We were spending a lot of time together at the office, and one day she confided in me that she had this problem, and that she was frightened. And I was…touched. All of those hidden emotions inside me came flooding out, directed toward her. I told myself all sorts of things. I told myself that lots of men have occasional affairs, that it means nothing, all the Hollywood clichés."

He smiles sheepishly for a second—probably thinking I'll find it endearing—and then goes on. "I told myself that you didn't need me as much as she did, and that anyway, you'd never find out. I told myself that my happiness depended on my having a kindred soul at the job. And that *your* happiness depended on *my* happiness. And I deluded myself into thinking that, because she was suffering, she was a kindred soul. I was disillusioned with the law. At least with the way it's practiced at big corporate firms like Burden, Lawrence, Shapiro, and O'Reilly. And Nicole was also disillusioned. She'd only gone into the law in the first place because her family expected her to. But she had no passion for it."

I feel resentful. Who's in therapy here, us or Nicole? Also, all his talk is starting to sound very rehearsed to me. But I've promised to hear him out. And I will. Even if it hurts, I'll hear it all.

"Nicole was dead inside. But drugs gave her the illusion of being alive. And I'd already stopped the physical side of things with her before you asked me. It was completely my decision. I'd stopped wanting her."

These words make me feel slightly better. Not much. Not enough. But slightly. *If* they're true. Well, I suppose they are. He seems to be past the lying stage, even if he's now into the well-rehearsed speechifying stage; but what would be the point of his lying to me any longer?

"But emotionally I was still entangled, still caught up in trying to save her. And," he adds dryly, "in case you're wondering where she is now, she's at a drug rehabilitation center."

I search my heart; can't I find it in myself to feel any sympathy for this poor little rich girl, this cokehead, who slept with my husband? Nope. Sorry. I can't. Does that make me a monster? Babette Frankenstein? Well, so be it. And is George a better person because he cared about her habit? If Nicole weren't tall and blond, would he have cared at all? He passes hundreds of less elegant drug addicts on the street every day, and he doesn't even say good morning to them. And anyway, I wonder what George intends to do with all of his newfound wisdom and self-awareness. This I _have_ to ask; I can't stop myself. "So what's your plan to save humanity, George?" I mutter through clenched teeth.

Dr. First stirs. He looks up. "Did you say something, Babette?"

I really _hate_ Dr. First. I lean forward violently, in an even more aggressive position, the way the _toughest_ of the tough boys back in high school used to, the ones who ended up being sent to reform schools. I refuse to repeat my question. I'm certain that George heard me, even if the impassive Dr. First didn't.

George looks irritated with me, but I can tell that he's determined to try to stay calm. I do, however, detect the slightest bit of sarcasm when he starts to answer. "My _plan_, Babette, is that I'm actively looking around for another job." I watch him rearrange his features again, and I watch him make a silent mental note to keep that sarcasm out of his voice. He goes on, "Currently, you should know, I'm contacting some smaller firms. Firms where the law still _means_ something." Now he sounds almost beatific. "Or maybe I'll even teach. I don't know. All I know for sure is that I've overstayed my tenure at Burden, Lawrence, Shapiro, and O'Reilly." His eyes are brimming over with honesty, and then he shrugs, which seems to indicate that he's finished for the moment.

I close my eyes to avoid his earnest gaze. With his sudden passion for truth and justice, George is starting to sound like someone on a soapbox, and I wonder whether he really believes in what he's saying, or whether it's simply a ploy to worm his way back into my heart. Still, even if he did rehearse some of what he's been saying, I have to be fair to him—it could just as well have been because he was nervous about trying to talk to me after so long in an unknown shrink's office, rather than because of some Machiavellian scheme he's hatched.

But, whichever it is, I'm not at all sorry to hear that he wants to find a new job. Because one of these days, Nicole is going to return from her "detoxificication/beauty spa," or wherever it is that rich girls go when they need some drying out, undoubtedly looking fit and fabulous. And whether or not George and I ever get back together again, I'd still rather he not be in the same office with her when she returns.

And I also have to wonder where all this leaves me. Because my dilemma is different from his. Mine boils down to that centuries-old query, to forgive or not to forgive, that is the question. In other words, to be able to accept a husband who's not the perfect Spiritual Beatle of a prepubescent's imagination, after all, and who's very confused and talking pop psychology in an attempt to understand himself, and who had the hots for another woman, as well as the nerve and insensitivity to act upon those hots, even though his wife *still* hasn't acted upon her own hots for other men, some of whom, like Carlos, are much, much nicer, and much more deserving of some good loving than Nicole ever was, that's for sure! So in other words, I have to decide whether to accept a much-less-than-perfect marriage that's going to need a hell of a lot of work in order for it to survive. I open my eyes and look over at the silent Dr. First. He's staring at his desk, as bland-looking as ever. He stirs, probably sensing my eyes on him. He looks up. "Fine, George," he says. "Babette, is there anything you'd like to say now?"

After all that George has revealed to me, I know that I should respond. But I'm still reeling from everything he's told me. I need some time alone to absorb it all. I turn back to George. He looks tense. I uncross my legs. I take a deep breath. "I…believe you," I say softly to George. And I *think* that I really mean it. I realize that it's still a far cry from I *forgive you*, but it's the best I can do.

"Thank you," George says. He's looking inscrutable again, and I can't tell whether he's angry, whether he thinks I'm being fair or unfair, generous or mean-spirited.

"I'm afraid that's all the time we have for today," Dr. First says. "Would you like to set up our next appointment?"

I can't bear the idea of seeing this man again. I don't care whether my feelings toward him are rational or not. The bottom line is that I can't stand him, his bland demeanor, his offensively inoffensive beige office, and that's that. "I'm sorry," I say, trying to sound as polite and controlled as he does, "I'm afraid I'm not ready to do that yet."

"Fine," Dr. First says, not revealing any emotion. He rises, and George and I follow his lead. He shakes George's hand, but not mine.

George and I walk out into the hallway and wait for the elevator together. I don't say anything, and he doesn't ask me why I don't want to see Dr. First again.

When the elevator comes—now featuring a Muzak version of Madonna's "Material Girl"—we both step inside. I ring for the lobby. As soon as the door closes, he says, "I couldn't stand him, either. Shara-Rose told me she thought it would be good for us to see someone very different from herself. Someone low-key."

"Low-key? He's a zombie."

George laughs, seeming much more at ease, far less rehearsed, and far more *real* to me than he had back in that unreal beige office. "Well," he says, "in any case, I think she was quite mistaken. Don't you?"

"Quite," I answer seriously, and I decide on the spot that I'm not interested in couple therapy, period. Not with Dr. First. And not with anyone. And, although this is undoubtedly blasphemy for a woman in her thirties living on the West Side of Manhattan, I think that I've had enough of therapy. Maybe Shara-Rose is onto something by leaving the profession. I feel a sense of freedom. For the moment, though, I keep this little epiphany to myself.

The elevator makes an unscheduled stop at the twelfth floor, and the door opens, but nobody gets on. When the door closes, to my complete surprise, George and I fall into each other's arms, making out like two horny teenagers. It happens so naturally that

I'm not even sure which of us started it. Well, just because we're still attracted to each other doesn't mean we should *be* together. Maya remained attracted to Merv for years after he'd left her for the showroom bimbo. "I can't help myself," she used to tell me, "he *is* the father of my child, after all." And I'll bet anything that Patti Boyd—even after she'd *voluntarily* allowed herself to be "stolen" by Eric Clapton—never got over her attraction to George Harrison. How could she have?

When the elevator reaches the lobby, we separate. The three doormen are staring at us. I blush, reminding myself that unless there are hidden cameras in the elevator, they couldn't possibly have seen us making out. Then again, in New York, anything is possible. And so what if they did? It'll be good for them, it'll help brighten up a boring day. Deliberately holding my head high, I walk past them and out into the street. George follows me.

"Let's share a cab to 57th Street," he offers, when we're in front of the building.

For some reason, I don't feel as though I can bear to be with him another minute. It's true that I am heading directly to 57th Street, to TAG, where I'm going to brave the presence of Sarah Burden and make phone calls to other arts organizations around the city to enlist their support for the demonstration. "I can't," I tell him. "I'm going to take the subway up to the Bronx. I have a sudden urge to see what my old neighborhood looks like these days." It's a pretty bizarre lie, and I'm sure that George knows it, although I can't tell from his expression whether he thinks I'm being amusing or infuriating. And I don't care. Despite our horny make-out session in the elevator, I really need to be alone.

He doesn't say a word. Instead, he kisses me lightly on the cheek. He turns, steps into the street, and sticks out his hand to hail a cab.

I start to walk away, resisting the temptation to turn around and look at him one last time. What I can't resist, though, is the temptation of hoping that *he's* turning around to look at me.

I head over to Broadway, where I stop into the first deli I come to, and I buy myself a pint of chocolate chocolate chip ice cream. Then I walk to the bus stop, joining the dozen or so people already waiting. They all look hot and disgruntled, as though they've been waiting for a long, long time.

I dig into the frozen ice cream with the feeble plastic spoon the guy at the deli counter gave me. I refuse to feel guilty about it. It's a pretty harmless addiction, after all. And I haven't gained any more weight. I must be burning up all the extra calories with frustration. Finally, the bus pulls up to the curb. I shove the nearly empty pint into the paper bag, hiding it from the driver, and I step on and find a seat in the back row. I ride down to 57th Street with my eyes closed, trying not to think about the fact that the little bit of ice cream that's left is probably melting like mad, since the bus is moving down Broadway at a pace that gives new meaning to the old phrase "a slow boat to China." I also try not to think about the fact that just a half hour ago, I was making out with my estranged husband in the elevator of a strange building. I try to think instead about TAG's imminent demonstration, and about which arts organizations I should call for support.

27

It's perfect demonstration weather, warm and sunny. I'm standing on the corner of 57th and Tenth, handing out picket signs. Despite my various personal crises, I'm feeling warm and sunny myself, geared-up, excited, and proud, even if we rate only a couple of cops who look alternately bemused and bored. I can't help but wonder whether our little demonstration is going to have the slightest effect at all.

Still, we're planning on doing all the traditional protest stuff. We're going to march up and down the block carrying protest signs, we're going to listen to inspiring speeches, and undoubtedly, at some point, we're all going to burst into "We Shall Overcome."

But in a way, it feels more like a high-school reunion than a protest rally. Long-lost friends are greeting each other, hugging and catching up on news. "So, are you working?" I hear a woman with teased blond hair, whom I recognize as FemmeDance's publicist, ask another woman. "No," the woman sighs, "just endlessly auditioning. What about you?" I can't hear the teased blond's response, because there's suddenly a traffic jam on the block, and the noise of the car horns is deafening. Also, Jay is standing on the make-shift little stage that he and I put together early this morning, and he's tapping on his microphone and waving his megaphone and bouncing up and down on the balls of his feet and pushing his slid-ing glasses up and down and shouting, "Testing, Testing!" every other second.

In addition to theater people, we've managed to attract painters and sculptors, a couple of East Village tenants' rights groups, a group of anarchist composers who are friends with the Microtonals, a small group of intense-looking writers and editors who know Pearl Green, the residents of the building next door to TAG, which probably also will be slated for doom soon, and a number of very angry and vocal artists who were displaced from their SoHo lofts when SoHo became gentrified, as well as friends and relatives who wouldn't ordinarily find themselves at something like this in a million years, except for the fact that someone they love is involved. I spot Jay's brother, an insurance salesman in Teaneck. And Maya, whom I haven't seen since we had our last "private talk" outside Jay's office. She's dressed in what I suspect she thinks is wild protest garb: a pink cape and leggings. She waves at me.

I wave back, and then I spot the Microtonals, and Doreen Cioffi, and Pearl Green, and Karl Ranger, who's so shy that Jay and I weren't able to persuade him to make a speech at the demonstra-tion about the plight of small businesses in the area. I wave at everyone, but the demand for picket signs has suddenly picked up, so I'm too busy to go over and chat. I'm very proud of our signs, which say, in big black letters, "Hell, No, The Arts Won't Go!" Jay and Sarah and I were up all last night making them. And due to a sudden surprising demand, Sarah is back upstairs at TAG, hurried-ly making some more. It's taken a great deal of effort on my part to work side by side with her, but I'm doing it for TAG's sake. And she does have a flair for making picket signs.

Some of the demonstrators have come prepared with their own signs. Some of the displaced SoHo artists are carrying signs that say, "New York, Culture Capital of the World," with a line through "Culture" and the word "Greed" substituted. And I spot a lone bald-headed man dressed all in black carrying a sign that says, "New York without the Arts Is Like a Picnic without the Ants!" which strikes me as an ambiguous message, to say the least.

An attractive young man appears at my side. He looks familiar. "Babette Bliss," he says, "you never called."

It's Trent Johnson. His blond ponytail has grown longer, and he's wearing a metallic-colored jacket and black jeans. "Glad you're here, Trent," I say, determined to stick to business, despite the fact that he's just as attractive in clothes as in a bathing suit. Even at a moment like this, right before the demonstration for TAG, I feel immediate desire for him. Well, it only goes to show— lusty female that I am—how lucky George has been that I never strayed. "Carry this," I tell Trent, trying to keep the desire out of my voice. I hand him a picket sign. He nods, salutes me flirtatiously, and wanders off, probably to try to find himself either a girl or an acting job in the crowd.

Our permit allows us to demonstrate from noon until two o'clock, which means that the demonstration is officially scheduled to begin in fifteen minutes, when all the media and business types on the block start hitting the summertime streets, ready for what they think will be their usual quiet lunch hour.

And now Jay is at my side, sweating profusely, pushing up his glasses, cracking his knuckles, and in general looking as though he's just swallowed a suitcase full of amphetamines. Jay, however, is one person who doesn't need speed in order to get wired. "Babette," he says urgently to me, "I want you to assume general responsibility for making sure that things go smoothly."

"Sure," I reply easily, because I don't expect things to go anything *but* smoothly at our peanut-size demonstration. I mean, even when all those artists in SoHo were evicted and displaced, I don't think anybody so much as suffered a bloody nose over it. And before that, when all the SoHo artists displaced all the small SoHo manufacturers, I didn't hear of any violence, either. On the other hand, I remind myself, there _were_ riots, not too long ago, over housing rights and squatters' rights in the East Village. So if it happened there, it could happen here. All it would take to turn today's demonstration into a riot would be one rock-throwing artist or one trigger-happy cop. Nervously, I look around. The artists all are busy adding little drawings to their picket signs, eating avocado sandwiches on pita bread, drinking sodas, and discussing who's been sleeping with whom at the various artists' colonies. I don't see a single rock. The two cops are busy getting Lydia Smart's autograph. Lydia, looking up, spots me watching her. We wave at each other. I'm really proud of her; she flew in from the Coast to be here today to lend her support. And she's flying right back out there at two o'clock. And that also pleases me, since it means that Carlos and I can continue to stay at her place.

Some of the homeless people from the public plaza on Ninth Avenue have joined the crowd, and they're asking everyone for halves of sandwiches and spare change and cigarettes. They have other things on their minds besides the fate of a group of artists who aren't able to afford space to work in. I don't blame them, since they can't even afford space to live in.

I look around for TV camera crews, but I see only one, from a small cable station. The crew consists of a few guys wearing Hawaiian shirts, eating grapes, and halfheartedly setting up their equipment.

It seems a shame that they're the only camera crew in sight, since there are two major TV stations on the block. Maybe we'll only be able to get our fair share of media coverage if there _is_ a riot, after all. Maybe I should throw a rock.

Jay appears by my side again. "We're set to go on in about three minutes," he cracks his knuckles, "and where are all the politicians who said they'd come by? And the newspapers? That's what I'd like to know!" He points to the cable TV crew, who are still eating their grapes. "What the hell do you have to do to be considered newsworthy in this town?"

I decide to keep quiet about throwing rocks, because Jay is liable to want me to do it.

Carlos drifts over, his mirrored sunglasses ablaze with sunlight.

"I know what we need," Jay goes on, ignoring me and Carlos. "We need an angle. A gimmick. A hook. Something that makes this demonstration different from all other demonstrations." He pauses, and then his eyes light up. He snaps his bony fingers. "We can use *them*," he points to a couple of homeless women who are leaning against a car, drinking Cokes and eating pita and avocado sandwiches. "We'll get all the homeless people from the plaza over here, and we'll give them each a couple of dollars to carry signs. We'll get Sarah to make some signs that say, 'I May Be Homeless, but I Care About the Arts!' Now, *that's* an angle!"

I'm appalled. "It's a disgusting angle."

"A really disgusting, exploitative angle," Carlos elaborates.

Jay shrugs.

"If you try it, I'll call off the demonstration," I say forcefully.

"I was only kidding," Jay says, not looking even slightly ashamed of himself. He looks at his watch. "Okay," he says, "we're on." He starts to walk toward the makeshift little stage. But he quickly turns around. "Oh, Babette," he says, "before I forget... find a minute during all this to talk to Maya. She's got something to say to you." And then he's gone, and I can't really worry about what Maya wants to say to me—she probably wants to have another "private talk" with me about my craziness—because Jay is on stage, and things are beginning to happen, and people on their lunch hours are starting to hang around, looking curious, and, in some cases, sympathetic, just as we hoped they would. The cable

TV cameras are rolling, and even the two cops are looking more alert.

The traffic jam is over, but I still can't hear everything that Jay is saying, because perky little Sarah's just come downstairs dragging a load of picket signs that looks as though it would give Arnold Schwarzenegger a hernia, and she and I are now busy handing them out together and answering the questions of onlookers.

"What the hell's going on here?" an elderly, slightly mad-looking woman asks us. Despite the heat, she's wearing a green velour turtleneck dress, a fur stole, and six inches of rouge on her cheeks, and she's carrying some sort of parasol.

I begin to explain to her what the demonstration is for, but a teenage messenger whizzes up on his bike. "What's going on here, lady?" he demands, bobbing his head up and down to the music from his Walkman.

So I start all over, but before I can get two words out of my mouth, a small crowd has gathered around me and Sarah, and they're all asking, "What's going on here?" and I can only make out bits and pieces of Jay's speech. "High rents," I hear him shout from the stage, and then he says something I can't make out, and then I hear, "low means!"

"Listen to that man onstage," I say desperately, pointing to Jay.

For the moment, at least, my little crowd falls silent, and Sarah wanders off to hand out signs at another location, and I'm able to make out an entire sentence of Jay's. "The cultural life of New York City," he shouts, "is enhanced by the presence of working artists!"

To my surprise and pleasure, the crowd breaks into spontaneous applause.

The teenage messenger taps me on the shoulder. "Why are they all clapping?"

"Ssh," I advise him, wishing he would turn down his Walkman, "listen."

"We need to put pressure on the real estate developers!" Jay cries.

At the words *real estate developers*, people hiss and boo, including the elderly woman in green velour.

"And on the so-called urban planners!"

At the words *urban planners*, they hiss and boo again. "Screw the motherfucking urban planners!" the teenage messenger shouts.

"We need legislative protection!" Jay says. People burst into applause again.

"Look what happened in SoHo!" Jay yells.

The displaced SoHo crowd goes wild. "Never again!" they shout fiercely, "never again!"

"Art brings employment and tourists to New York! Artists are workers! And like all workers, we need affordable space to do our work!"

"Declare this building a landmark!" someone in the crowd shouts out.

There's a smattering of applause for this idea, but I sincerely doubt that the Landmarks Preservation Commission would go for it. It's just a cruddy-looking, poorly maintained nonentity of a tenement, which used to be a piano factory. I feel a lump in my throat, and I wonder for the first time whatever happened to the piano factory people. Were they displaced, too? Like us, was their lease about to expire, and did they have no legal recourse? Did TAG, in fact, put the workers from the piano factory out on the street? And does that make me a part of the problem instead of the solution? I feel very sad, and angry at myself that I've never even thought about this until now.

"Hell, no, the arts won't go!" are Jay's parting words as he steps down from the stage to a hearty round of applause.

The applause that greets Lydia, however, as she steps up to the stage, is heartier than hearty: it's tumultuous, bordering on lunatic. I still can't quite believe it. Lydia, who just a few years ago couldn't fill TAG's small auditorium, is now a full-fledged star, thanks to that Artists for the Arts Fellowship. Well, star or not, she looks very simple and demure today. She's gained a little weight, so maybe she's up to a hundred and five pounds, she's dyed her short hair a shimmery silver color, and she's wearing a sleeveless madras shift and flat leather sandals.

"Please," Lydia holds up her hand to stop the applause. "I'm here today because it's important to me to take a stand for TAG, because TAG, which means Jay Adroit and Babette Bliss, gave me my first break." She smiles down at Jay, and then in my direction. I feel embarrassed, and I hope that nobody is looking at me. Taking a quick peek around, I'm both relieved and disappointed to see that nobody is. All eyes remain on Lydia.

"It would be a crime," Lydia says passionately, "if TAG and the other artists and groups in the building didn't survive." She pauses for audience applause. The camera crew and the cops are paying rapt attention. I spot a second camera crew setting up.

Lydia plants her feet firmly apart. Then she closes her eyes. People are smiling excitedly, because these are her trademark gestures, her cues to her audience that she's about to perform. And sure enough, a second later she opens her eyes, her whole body shakes uncontrollably, and she begins to shriek, taking on the voice of an angry homeless woman: "Ain't got no roof over my head! And I ain't going to no shelter, either! You know, they rape women in the shelters! You know, they kill people in the shelters!" She fixes her gaze on the audience. "And the newspapers, they tell you all to pass me by, to turn me down, when I ask you for spare change. But don't pass me by, people. I need your spare change!" And she begins to shout, over and over, "Spare Change! Spare Change!" and the crowd is shouting along with her. Even the homeless are shouting along. "Spare Change! Spare Change! Spare Change!"

It's thrilling, and terrifying, too, to see her arouse and inspire the crowd like this, although even now, in the midst of this frenetic shouting, I can't get rid of the notion that all of our good intentions and camaraderie here today aren't going to do a thing. But before I can dwell too long on that, I spot Shara-Rose's curly red hair in the crowd. She's wearing that girlish white outfit again, which must mean her mother's still visiting from Florida, and she's shouting, "Spare Change! Spare Change!" along with everyone else. She looks up and spots me. She waves. Hesitantly, I wave back. I'm touched that she's come to the demonstration to show her support. Although I'm still a little angry at her for giving up her practice during my time of crisis. But I feel something else, too. Something contradictory. I feel relieved. Because that little epiphany I had in the elevator of Dr. First's building really *was* true: I have had enough of therapy. At least for the present. And I notice who's standing on either side of Shara-Rose. On her left is Ronnie, her waiter-actor-lover, whom I haven't seen since the evening at Tarts. And on her right is George, dressed casually in jeans and a short-sleeved shirt, which means he's taken another day off from work. He's not shouting, "Spare Change!" Instead, he's looking right at me. Confused, I look back up at Lydia.

"And now," Lydia says, abruptly stopping her shouting, "I'm going to invite a good friend of mine up here to join me: Carlos Carlos!"

Carlos climbs onstage. "Yo, Carlos!" someone shouts out. He's carrying his guitar, and he and Lydia begin to sing Bob Dylan's old protest song, "Blowing in the Wind," and everyone joins in. Even the teenage messenger sings along, although he seems to think the words are "The answer my friend, is Burger King...."

From out of nowhere, it seems, Maya has appeared in front of me, blocking my view of Lydia and Carlos. I nod at her, but I don't stop singing. "Babette," she says, "I need to talk to you."

She's blushing so much that her cheeks almost match her cape. She slips her arm through mine. I stop singing and stare at her. It isn't like Maya to blush. Or, at least, to blush sincerely, which I think is what she's doing. "Jay and I are getting married," she says.

The elderly woman in green velour pats her on the shoulder. "Lucky girl," she says.

But I'm speechless. I feel a completely stupid, flycatching expression come over my face. I just stare at her.

She disengages her arm from mine. Her blush is fading. Somehow, I manage to say it. "Congratulations," I mutter grimly, looking down at the ground.

"Thank you," she says coolly, obviously not satisfied. She turns her attention to the stage, where Jay has joined Lydia and Carlos.

I also turn my attention to Jay, Lydia, and Carlos, who, with their linked arms, look like an avant-garde Peter, Paul, and Mary. I wonder if they're about to sing "If I Had a Hammer." But they have other things on their minds. "People, let's march!" Jay shouts. "Let's show this town who the streets and the buildings really belong to!"

At first the crowd goes wild, and the anarchist composers start shouting the old sixties slogan "The streets belong to the people!" and I hope that things aren't about to get out of control. But everyone calms down, and, in a very orderly fashion, the march begins.

Still, I'm becoming more and more convinced, with every moment, that marching back and forth along 57th Street between Tenth and Eleventh avenues just isn't going to be that effective. And I hope that not too many people tire early and drop out to get a beer at Armstrong's. But so far, at least, there's no evidence of anyone tiring. "Hell, no, the arts won't go!" people are chanting as they march.

Maya and I are still standing awkwardly together on the corner of Tenth. We're not chanting and we're not marching.

"I've got to go meet a client in SoHo who's redoing her loft," Maya tells me, still sounding very miffed at me, and not even hearing the terrible irony of her words.

How, I wonder, will their marriage ever last? And how will Alex fare with her crazy Uncle Jay suddenly becoming her crazy Stepdaddy Jay? Well, Merv, her real father, is no bargain either, and she seems relatively unaffected by him, so maybe she'll be okay. And she'll have me to turn to, her blue Aunt Babette, for whatever it's worth. I hope that it's worth a lot. "Listen, Maya," I force myself to say, "I'm so beside myself about you and Jay getting married that I can hardly stand it. Really." It's the best I can do, and I only can hope that Maya, who, after all, was never an English major at Yale, isn't going to deconstruct my text.

She isn't. Instead, she smiles broadly at me, clearly satisfied by my words, and we kiss each other, although she kisses the air next to my cheek, which she always does in order to avoid smudging her lipstick.

And, just as I expected, the marching crowd, picket signs held aloft, has burst into "We Shall Overcome." Everyone, even the teenage messenger and the elderly woman in green velour, sounds as sweet and mournful as Joan Baez.

I get teary-eyed, and I look around for George. He undoubtedly will be interested to learn that he's about to gain a brother-in-law, estranged though he and I may be. I spot Shara-Rose and Ronnie in the crowd, marching and singing, but I don't see George with them. I look around for a minute or two longer, and then I give up. He must have left.

I join the march. And I begin to sing, startling myself because I, too, sound just like Joan Baez.

28

It's three o'clock. An hour since the demonstration ended. Jay, Carlos, Sarah, and I are sitting in Armstrong's. Our collective mood is somber and hushed: The Post-Demonstration Blues. Even Jay has an uncharacteristically reflective expression on his face.

None of us has spoken a word since we ordered. Jay, Sarah, and I are moodily nursing our beers. Carlos, who has to get back to his cab soon, is moodily nursing a cup of coffee.

I don't know what's going through anyone's else's mind, but the same five things keep going through mine. And always in the same order, too.

1) We did it, we pulled off a successful demonstration!
2) Our successful demonstration won't change a thing.
3) Whatever happened to those piano factory workers?
4) Will Jay and Maya really get married?
5) Where did George disappear to during the demonstration?

Finally, Sarah breaks the silence, interrupting the neat little pattern of my thoughts. In an achingly sweet Joan Baez–like voice, she begins to sing, "We Shall Overcome."

I must admit that the idea of a perky little rich girl singing in the voice of the oppressed is a bit hard to take. Even a well-meaning perky little rich girl with a fetching gap between her two front teeth. On the other hand, who am I to judge? What do I really know about oppression, either? These days I'm sitting pretty enough, married to a corporate lawyer. Even if the corporate lawyer and I currently are estranged. And even if the corporate lawyer currently is experiencing a massive attack of self-doubt and humanity. In any case, Sarah sings an entire verse and chorus, and none of us interrupt. But none of us join in, either.

After she finishes singing, I politely wait a moment, and then I speak. There's something I need to ask Jay. It's a question that's closely related to thought number two on my list, the one about the demonstration not doing a thing. "Jay, we all believe that demonstrating was the right thing to do," I begin, warming myself up to ask my question, "because it made our cause better known. And not just our cause, but the more general cause of the many people who aren't able to afford to work and live in this crazy city anymore."

Carlos removes his sunglasses, rubs his eyes, and looks at me as though I'm being too naive for words.

I ignore Carlos, and I ask Jay the question I have to ask. "But what if, after all this, the building still goes? What then?" This is the unvoiced question that has been on all of our minds all week long, I'm sure, as we prepared for the demonstration. It's as though we feared that if we voiced it, we would jinx things. But the demonstration is now history, and I hope very strongly that Jay has some kind of an answer.

"I'm glad you asked that." His voice is level. Thoughtful. Calm. Not at all manic. A voice designed to inspire confidence. "Doreen Cioffi and I have been talking about trying to get a bunch of arts organizations together to buy a building. It won't be easy, since nobody has any cash. But it's a possibility." He pauses. "Another possibility," he continues in that same calm, deliberate voice, "is to find a generous private patron who'll buy us a loft building."

Carlos snorts. It's a sarcastic-sounding snort, clearly intended to let us know exactly what he thinks TAG's chances of finding such a patron are.

"It's been done before, Carlos," Jay replies to the snort, still very calmly. "In the sixties, for example..."

"Ah, the lost, idealistic sixties," Carlos says melodramatically.

"In the sixties," Jay goes on, ignoring Carlos, "such things did occur now and then. And there's no reason to think it couldn't happen now. The Burdens, for example," Jay turns to Sarah, "own some real estate, don't they?" Butter, as the old cliché goes, could melt in Jay's mouth.

Sarah looks as though she's going to choke.

Carlos and I exchange knowing looks. We both turn to look at Jay, who's looking calmly at Sarah. But Sarah is staring into her glass of beer. "It's true," she says in a tiny voice, addressing the beer, "a few buildings. Somewhere. I'm not even sure where."

Jay pushes his eyeglasses up and turns his attention back to his own beer. He's much too smart to push her. He'll give her time to think about it on her own. To wrestle with her conscience, until she makes her decision about how best to approach Mummy and Daddy Burden with her request. "Just one itty-bitty building for some friends of mine," I can imagine her asking, smiling an endearing gap-toothed smile, "pretty please?" There's no guarantee, of course. The Burdens are not a family noted for their philanthropy. Sarah's cousin Nicole, for one, is a prime example of that. Still, it's no more farfetched than a group of struggling little out-of-the-mainstream arts organizations pooling together their meager resources and buying a building in Manhattan.

"Well," Carlos says, standing, "this has been a fascinating afternoon in more ways than one. But now, I must," he grins mischievously at Sarah, "rejoin the working class." He points a finger at me. "And don't forget, Babette. We have a date tonight."

"Oh, are you two going to work on *Hard-Boiled* tonight?" Sarah asks eagerly, looking up from her beer, sounding more like her perky self. She's probably glad to have an opportunity to change the subject from the Burden family's real estate holdings to my budding career as an artist.

Carlos nods. "And we're also going to work on a new piece called *The Flat Earth Society Takes Manhattan.*"

I cringe. It's true that Carlos and I have been tossing ideas back and forth about a crazy farce in which the last remaining octogenarian members of the Flat Earth Society stage a coup and take over the New York City government. But I wish Carlos hadn't mentioned it in front of Jay and Sarah. I still feel too much like an imposter posing as an artist, although Carlos assures me that the Imposter Syndrome is as *au courant* as narcissism. "Really, Babette," he keeps insisting, reminding me of Shara-Rose, "people have written books about it. Nobody knows why they're doing anything any longer. Half the people in the U.S. feel as though they're pretending to be something they're not. There are imposter plumbers. Imposter doctors. Just look at me, I'm an imposter cabbie."

Carlos leaves some money on the table for his coffee. "Later," he says to me.

I stare across the table at Jay, who's beginning to look manic again, and I remember what I'm obligated to do. "Jay," I say, reluctantly, holding my beer glass high, wishing that I were drinking vodka instead of beer so that the words might flow faster, "a toast to you and your upcoming marriage. Congratulations!" Now I really lay it on thick. "And welcome to the Bliss family!"

Jay grins, and he touches his beer glass to mine.

I lean over and embrace him, which strikes me as the sort of thing a loving sister-in-law-to-be should do to her loving brother-in-law-to-be.

"Wow, congratulations, Jay," Sarah chimes in, sounding genuinely enthusiastic. She's probably mostly enthusiastic because this means that Jay, obsessed with saving TAG though he may be, will have something else on his mind to distract him from his quest for a wealthy patron. Still, the thought occurs to me that a perfect wedding present from Sarah to Jay would be a new home for TAG. I'm sure that the same thought is occurring to Jay. I hope that it's also occurring to Sarah.

"It's too bad Maya couldn't join us here for a beer," I add, "but, as I'm sure you already know, she had an appointment to redecorate the apartment of a _fabulously_ rich client who owns a loft down in SoHo." I don't know for a fact that Maya's client is fabulously rich, but it's a good bet that she's not poor, that's for sure. Tensely, I wait for Jay's reaction to this news of Maya's whereabouts, because I need to see with my own eyes that Jay understands how mismatched he and Maya are, and that he loves her for who she really is. I feel protective of her. She's my sister, after all, and I want to make sure that Jay doesn't turn against her after the wedding when it sinks in that she's a bit...ditzy...to put it as kindly as I can. Despite Maya's "private talks" with me, I know she's still capable of being very, very hurt in love. In fact, most of the people I know are hurting a lot of the time when it comes to romance, even though, on the surface, everyone appears so cool and blasé about love and infidelity. Even I, who once was _truly_ cool and blasé about it, no longer am. The truth is that people—even narcissists and ditzy dames—have feelings. And feelings get hurt, even if nobody likes to admit it anymore.

Jay leans forward, pushing up those eternally sliding eyeglasses. "Your sister," he says to me, almost rapturously, "is the most complicated woman I've ever met!"

So that's his answer. Which, translated, means, "Love is blind."

I sigh. I rest my case. Jay will soon become my brother-in-law, and that's that. I wish the two of them only the best as they struggle through marriage together. Because it sure is a struggle, as I've come to know firsthand.

The waitress brings us the check.

"It's on me," Sarah announces eagerly.

Neither Jay nor I try to stop her. I hope this is a sign of bigger and better acts of generosity to come.

Outside Armstrong's, we separate. Jay and Sarah head back to TAG, but I decide to go back to Lydia's, to give Flaca, whom I've been neglecting in the recent demonstration madness, a little attention, and then to take a hot bath. Being a political activist is hard work, and I'm exhausted.

I cross Tenth Avenue, and start walking east along 57th, in the direction of Lydia's. But when I get to my building—that is, the building where I lived happily with George once upon a time not so very long ago—I stop in my tracks. As though it's the most natural thing in the world for me to be doing, I walk into the lobby.

Shyly, I ask Herman, the doorman, for the building's spare set of keys to my apartment. He smiles and hands them to me, not mentioning the fact that he hasn't seen me in quite a while. I thank him, and ring for the elevator.

When I get upstairs, I let myself in. I half expect George to come racing toward me, wielding some makeshift weapon, thinking that a burglar is breaking in. But he doesn't. Maybe he's not home.

Stealthily, I walk toward the bedroom. I can hear the noisy air-conditioner going. Either he forgot to turn it off when he went out this morning, or he's in there.

The bedroom door is open a crack, and I have this horrible image of my opening the door to find George and Nicole in bed together, naked, snorting coke, and making mean-spirited jokes about avant-garde playwrights/arts administrators who barely earn any money. It's the kind of image I still torment myself with, but it's also the kind of image that I have every intention of banishing from my imagination as quickly as possible. Because the bottom line is that I'm not someone who derives pleasure from self-torture, although these days I've been doing more than my fair share of it, I guess.

Very quietly, I open the door a crack further. I see the top of George's head. He's alone, under the covers, asleep. Which solves the mystery of where he disappeared to during the demonstration. Elementary, my dear Watson: He went home to catch forty winks. Which sounds like a damned good idea to me.

George has always been a sound sleeper. I tiptoe over to the bed. Or should I say, to *my* bed. Or better yet, to *our* bed. He doesn't wake up. He's all the way over to one side of the bed. My side of *our* bed.

Gingerly, I sit on the edge of the bed. I hold my breath. But he doesn't stir. As gently as I can, I lift the covers, swing my legs up, and lie down next to him. The bed—*our* bed—creaks slightly. I take a quick peek at him beneath the covers. All he's wearing is a pair of brightly checked red-and-white boxer shorts. I know these boxer shorts well, because I bought him five pairs exactly like this one about a year ago on impulse at one of those discount stores on lower Fifth Avenue. When I first gave them to him, tied up in a red ribbon, he looked at me incredulously, but, like a good sport, he's been wearing them ever since.

I close my eyes.

When I awaken, he's sitting up, leaning against the headboard, looking at me. He seems completely alert, so he's probably been up for a while. Before I can even yawn and rub my eyes and begin to acclimate myself, he takes me in his arms and begins to kiss me. I can tell that he's already feeling desirous and aroused. But I'm not. In fact, now that I'm waking up, what I'm feeling isn't desire or arousal at all. It's contentment. I feel absolutely content just lying here quietly in my own bed. *Our* bed, I mean. It's like running unexpectedly into an old and dear friend.

George stops kissing me, and he lies down next to me again, his warm shoulder touching mine. He seems to sense my mood, and I like the fact that he does. Maybe we can still, despite what's happened, be in perfect harmony.

"Do you want to talk?" he asks, after a minute.

"No," I answer bluntly, more than a little disappointed that he's already destroying our silent harmony. The very last thing I want to do at this moment is talk. About anything. I certainly don't want to talk about something trivial, like what we should have for dinner tonight. And I also don't want to talk about anything less trivial. There are so many things we're going to have to talk about, ad nauseam, and I'd like to put off talking about all of them for the moment. Things like his infidelity, which, as far as I'm concerned, needs a lot more explaining. And things like my own fidelity, which was pretty shaky there for a while, and—if I'm going to be absolutely honest with myself—may *still* be shaky for a while to come, while I'm collaborating with Carlos Carlos, even if we're no longer living together and I'm no longer parading around in my provocative shorts. Still, it will require *a lot* of vigilance on my part to maintain my monogamous stance, after all that has happened, and try as I might—and I *will* try—it ain't gonna be easy.

Also, down the road, George and I are going to have to talk about the fact that he *really* is going to have to get the hell out of Burden, Lawrence, Shapiro, and O'Reilly if he wants to stay married to me. And then, one of these days, we'll have to have a serious talk about my insecure-but-budding career as a playwright in the world of nonlucrative avant-garde theater, and how that's changing who I am. And also, although he hasn't yet expressed it to me, one day there'll have to be the talk about how furious he is at me for going so long without even giving him the courtesy of a chance to speak to me. And then there's still going to have to be a discussion—probably many, in fact—about whether or not we'll ever have children. So much talking to do! I'm exhausted just thinking about it.

It also occurs to me that a moment like this is exactly the kind of moment in which a couple could easily say, "Yes, yes, we'll conceive a child right now to symbolize our renewed marriage!" And of course, nine months later, when the little symbol comes kicking and squalling into the world, the marriage is on the rocks. I promise myself that that's one trap I'm not going to fall into.

"Okay," George says, "no talk."

We lie quietly again. I try to get back into my contented mood. To savor just being here in my own bedroom again. To savor the silence.

"Do you want to listen to some music?" he asks.

I sigh. I'm just going to have to accept the fact that he's in a completely different mood than I am, and that, for once, he's the one who's bugged by silence. So much for perfect harmony. "Sure, why not?" I give in, reminding myself that marriage is, after all, about compromise. In fact, maybe that's the real meaning of harmony in marriage. Constant, unrelenting, annoying compromise.

He rises from the bed, and he heads off into the living room to choose an album. I close my eyes and try to guess which album he'll choose. Something classical, I hope. Something timeless, elegant, and romantic. On the other hand, he's likely to choose a Beatles album, considering his recent penchant for singing Beatles songs. Well, that would be okay, too. One of their love songs would be nice.

He's back, and I hear him across the room fiddling with the old record player we keep on a shelf above his bureau.

I sit up and open my eyes. He turns the record player on. I'm horrified to hear the twangy country-'n'-western voice and guitar of Merle Haggard. I can't imagine anything less appropriate than Merle singing "Okie from Muskogee," the old, infamous antihippie, antipolitical protests anthem. I gaze at George in horror. Is he mocking TAG? And our reconciliation? And me? I feel ready to flee the room, to flee from this absurd pretense at saving our marriage. I want to hand him back to his coke-addicted Ice Queen and to buy myself some comforting ice cream instead. I want to fling myself into some other man's arms—Carlos or Trent, or the cute cabdriver the night we went to Tarts, or some unknown man, someone who looks like the *new* breed of rock stars, the ones from L.A. and Seattle, nothing like a Beatle. I want to start all over again, with no idealizing fantasies of any Beatles ever, *ever* allowed.

He's still standing by the record player and smiling sweetly at me. "This is so good to hear," he says.

I'm listening hard, but I don't detect any mockery in his voice.

"It reminds me of my childhood," he goes on. "All the farmers with their radios tuned to country-'n'-western stations all day long...."

He's not even hearing the words of the song. At this moment, Merle's political message is the farthest thing from George's mind. The only message George is getting is personal, and it has a lot more to do with the sound of Merle's deep and husky twang than with his words. George is simply remembering the innocence of his boyhood. Before his job at Burden, Lawrence, Shapiro, and O'Reilly, before he met me, before he met Nicole, before he hurt me, and before I walked out on him and hurt him. I purse my lips. He and I are, I have to face it, a long, long way from being in perfect harmony. Despite what the poets say, our two hearts are not beating as one. I resist the urge to get up and smash the Merle Haggard album to pieces. I lean forward. "Okay, listen," I say, "I forgive you." And *I forgive me, too*, I think, *for being a little bit crazy*, although I don't say it aloud.

I lean back against the headboard.

He hums along with Merle.